# THE LAST POKÉMON MASTER

# THE LAST POKÉMON MASTER

### AN UNOFFICIAL
## POKÉMON GO
### ADVENTURE

## CAROL CHRISTO
### TRANSLATION BY DANIEL HAHN

DINO

Published by John Blake Publishing Ltd
3 Bramber Court, 2 Bramber Road,
London W14 9PB, England

www.johnblakebooks.co.uk
www.facebook.com/johnblakebooks 
twitter.com/jblakebooks 

First published in paperback in 2016
ISBN: 978 1 78606 387 8

British Library Cataloguing-in-Publication Data:
A catalogue record for this book is available from the British Library.

Design by www.envydesign.co.uk

Printed in Great Britain by CPI Group (UK) Ltd

1 3 5 7 9 10 8 6 4 2

© Text copyright Carol Christo 2016

The right of Carol Christo to be identified as the author of this work has been
asserted by her in accordance with the Copyright, Designs and Patents Act 1988.

Papers used by John Blake Publishing are natural, recyclable products made from
wood grown in sustainable forests. The manufacturing processes conform to the
environmental regulations of the country of origin.

Every attempt has been made to contact the relevant copyright-holders,
but some were unobtainable. We would be grateful if the
appropriate people could contact us.

*To my godson Lucas,*
*who also wanted to be a*
*Pokémon Master one day*

# CONTENTS

# CHAPTER 1

# A VERY BAD DECISION

**W**hen it happened for the first time, I thought I was going crazy. I was not astonished, nor did I feel particularly special. The only thing I could think of was that I was definitely losing my mind.

If you, like me, also dream of becoming a Pokémon Master, I suggest you listen to me carefully: choose something else for your life. And I don't say this because becoming a Pokémon Master is something impossible. It's actually quite the opposite. I say it because the things we most want to happen, in one way or another, usually do. So I repeat: find yourself a safer dream. Dream about being a doctor, a teacher, an astronaut, anything not involving powerful little monsters, as that outcome may be disastrous.

My name is Lucas and, like you, I had started playing

1

this new game. After all, I *am* the most Pokémon-addicted person I know. I am a typical ten-year-old, spending my time playing games online and on video game consoles. I have amassed a large collection of games throughout my whole life. I cannot say this makes my parents very happy, but as long as my results in school are as good as my best friend Samuel's are, then it's okay. I think that, despite everything, my mum and dad are proud of me.

You might have noticed: when the game came out, it was the most important thing in the world. At least that's how things seemed in Year Six.

Cora, Samuel, and I were ready. We knew that whatever it was, it was going to be bigger this time, because we were talking about Pokémon here, and for the time being, there was nothing official being released anywhere else, nothing that was truly worthwhile or different. It was already night-time when the app became available in the UK, and Samuel, who doesn't own a smartphone despite being a programming genius (as well as a genius in other fields), had to beg to use his mother's phone. But this proved to be unsuccessful as she always forgot to recharge her mobile's battery so we couldn't get online.

Once we logged into the game, we spent weeks hunting Pokémon every free minute we had. In the early hours, before school, during the breaks, after school ... We found several Pokémon around the neighbourhood and the school. Samuel, who is tall and thin, and is used to running around, now used his speed to catch Pokémon. But Cora, whose parents never let her go out alone, would only play when we were all together. I, in my somewhat-poor physical condition, was always lagging behind them both. Our collection of captured little monsters was growing ever larger, but finding different specimens from those we already had was becoming harder and harder. It was then that we made a radical decision. And I have to tell you, I have always been a lousy decision-maker.

There we were, trying to sneak out through the school's back gate, eager to capture as many creatures as possible during the five-and-a-half hours in which we should have been studying maths, English, science, and whatever else we had to do on Wednesdays. There was a rumour going around that a Gyarados had popped up at the local park, and if it was true, then a lot was at stake. A Gyarados was something special, and, though I was a diligent player, I had never found one. The aim was set, and the plan defined. It was finally time for our Pokémon adventure to begin.

\* \* \*

These are times when it's seriously fun to be ten years old. My father said he used to bunk off school when he was this age to play soccer. Well, I was skipping classes for the first time in my life, only I was using my illicit breaks to catch Pokémon. Truly, I think that, by comparison, I had the better deal. Soccer, you see, is an unbearable thing for me.

I was excited about the game that day, my adrenaline

level was high, and I even did pretty well with some training battles in a friendly gym that morning. I also memorised the names of all Pokémon, including the rare ones. My only problem is that while I'm brave in the virtual world, I find the real world much more complicated.

'Here, Lucas!' shouted Cora, while she acted as a lookout so that Samuel could cross the playground without being noticed. Her long hair was tied up in a high ponytail.

'Act normal, man,' whispered Samuel. 'You look as if you've just committed a crime. If you go on like that, we won't get past Virgil, the security guard, even if we had a note from our parents.'

'It's all right!' I said as we squatted behind some nearby pillars. It wasn't my fault that I'd never bunked off school before.

'I just want to remind you how much money you'll need, because the bus ticket is £2.20. I hope you two remembered this.'

'What?' I shouted.

'I have ten pounds that my godfather gave me yesterday, so I'm all set,' said Samuel.

'Hey, you're only telling us about the fare now? That's so not okay!' I complained. 'You should have told us earlier.'

'Lucas, I hate to say this to you,' Cora shot back, 'and it's not because I am a girl. But I'm not here to play the role of your mother, okay?'

'Okay, but when you ask me to help you evolve your Bulbasaur, I will remind you of this conversation, *Mummy*.'

'I don't need your help to evolve anything, okay?' Cora

4

turned her face away, looking like someone who'd heard something they didn't want to hear.

Well, everybody knows that I'm the Pokémon expert of the group.

'Hey, you guys. I don't want to cause panic or anything, but … Virgil saw us and is coming this way.' Samuel nudged Cora, who turned to see the security guard walking toward us. I couldn't decide whether to run, cry, or hide behind Samuel, because I'm pretty bad at making excuses.

'Hey, there is a Meowth behind him,' said Cora excitedly, looking at the guard via the screen of her mobile phone. 'Just wait a second. I'm going to–' But she never got a chance to finish the sentence, as we were yanked away by Samuel.

We ran like crazy toward the basketball court. I didn't know I could run so fast.

'Hey, you made me lose that Meowth!' Cora shouted while we walked across the courtyard and towards the gate.

'Look, I could have left you there to spend the day in the headmaster's office, but that would have ruined our plans,' answered Samuel.

'Do you think Virgil saw us?' I asked.

'Nah,' answered Cora, pointing her phone around and scanning in every direction. 'Look, he's over there talking with some Year Eights, so we can relax. I could have *caught* that Meowth.' She frowned and looked at Samuel, who just shrugged his shoulders in response.

When we got to the gate, I was already out of breath.

Don't misunderstand me, I'm no wimp, but physical exercise is not my strong suit. Although things had been improving since Cora, Samuel, and I had been walking all over the neighbourhood for the last few days.

'A-ha!' said Cora, grabbing the gate triumphantly, as though she were the smartest girl around. 'I knew it would be unlocked, since this is where they take the rubbish bins out and today's collection day.'

Then she pushed open the gate and we went out, carefully, trying to walk like ordinary people who were not doing anything wrong.

I checked Twitter and confirmed the rumours about the Gyarados at the city park, so we walked towards the bus stop, seeking the one Pokémon that, although we didn't realise it, would turn our world upside down. Oh, if I had known what was about to happen, I'm sure I would have gladly gone back to the maths class.

## CHAPTER 2

# NOBODY EVER BELIEVES ME

It was Monday morning and the inhabitants of the park were mostly people jogging or running. Don't ask me how someone was able to wake up at six or seven in the morning and do that. But, well, to each their own.

Along the way, we found several Pokémon, including a Flareon and an Onix that my friends could hardly capture because of its high Combat Power (also known as CP). I had to go back to some gyms and increase my level as fast as possible if I wanted to be strong enough to capture all of them. I also needed to improve my Charmander by getting more stardust and candy for him. I was especially fond of my lizard Pokémon, as it had been my first, and I'd decided to increase his level to maximum. My Charmander was going to be my faithful shield-bearer now. I also wanted to have the necessary power to capture all the legendary

Pokémon, but so far, I had not heard of anyone even having found one of them.

Cora was all happy with her Jigglypuff, and Samuel was on the other side of the lake, where a Blastoise had popped up. My Pokémon count kept rising, and it was still before eight in the morning. I just knew that this was going to be a good day; I could feel it.

You know, sometimes I get knocked backwards by my naïveté, because as soon as I thought about how awesome the day was going to be, a fierce wind blew down a giant pine tree in front of me. *Right in front of me!* It was just pure chance that I was alive, what with that fallen giant tree about ten inches away from my feet. I had never witnessed anything like that. I mean, strong winds during storms were quite common in the area, but not on a sunny spring morning!

'Gosh!' shouted Cora from behind, with her hands on her chest to calm her racing heartbeat.

'Hey, boy,' called Samuel, 'you always say you have no luck, but look. That was a close call!'

I guess that was one way of seeing things...

'Guys, I think this is a sign for us to go back to school,' I said, being the sensible person I am.

Cora was still looking on in amazement at the fallen pine tree when she said, 'But, Lucas – *you're* the one who had the idea of bunking off school!' Samuel added, completing her sentence. 'For goodness sake, I even asked if you really meant it!'

I stood there motionless, looking at that huge tree,

wondering if it was really worth doing all this if it involved all these risks.

'Look! There's a Venonat near the flowers!' announced Cora. She and Samuel quickly ran to the other side of the park in search of the poisonous Pokémon. I kept standing in the same place until I noticed something weird happening in the park's lake: a whirlpool was forming near the edge, close to the small bridge that crossed it.

'Hey, guys!' I called out, approaching the lake. 'Guys?' I said again, but they were too far away to hear me. It was at this moment that the whirlpool on the water rose about fifteen feet into the air. I tried to scream, but no sound came out of my mouth.

I couldn't get away from it in time, and the whirlpool suddenly span apart into nothingness, but not before leaving me completely soaked. One thing was for sure: my day was not improving. I was so shocked by what had happened that I remained motionless, until I saw Cora and Samuel walking in my direction.

'Lucas, what happened?' asked Cora. 'My goodness, where's your mobile? Is it wet?'

'Man, didn't anyone ever tell you this water isn't good for swimming?' fired Samuel.

'My mobile, Cora? Are you worried about … my mobile? A HURRICANE OF WATER JUST ROSE UP AND THREW ITSELF AT ME AND YOU WANT TO KNOW ABOUT MY MOBILE?!' I shouted at her.

What kind of friends were these?

Cora got closer and put her hand on my forehead.

'Are you feeling okay?' she asked.

'He must have eaten something rotten,' joked Samuel.

'Something weird happened in the lake!' I told them. 'There was a whirlpool about fifteen feet high!' It became a little clearer to me why nobody ever took me seriously.

'He is totally nuts,' said Cora, sitting down on a park bench near the fallen pine tree.

'First a pine tree falls right in front of you, then there's a giant whirlpool … This day is just full of surprises,' said Samuel.

'Okay, okay. I'm used to it by now. You guys never really believe me.' I fumbled in my pocket for my phone. At least in that regard, I wasn't a complete fool. My mobile's case was totally waterproof. Cora took it from my hand as I sat beside her.

'Phew!' she said while she fumbled through my apps. 'At least the phone is intact. You should go to the far side of the park. I caught a Kabuto and a Chansey over there.'

'What I really want is that Gyarados,' I said to her. 'Have you seen any around here?'

Cora peered at her own phone's screen.

'It looks like there's one in the outer perimeter. I think by the other side of the lake, over there,' she said while gesturing.

'Then let's go there,' I said to both of them.

We headed to the opposite side of the lake, holding up our mobiles and watching for any approaching Gyarados. I wasn't aware of, or at least couldn't pinpoint, the reason why I was suddenly feeling a shiver creep down my spine.

Sometimes in life we try to convince ourselves that certain things are normal, for instance strong trees being blown down by passing winds and whirlpools appearing out of nowhere and crashing over people. We convince ourselves that so many highly unusual things are normal that it's difficult to separate something commonplace from those rare coincidences that might suggest something much more significant is happening.

I used to be the type of person that paid attention to warning signs within myself, such as chills or shivers down my spine that seemed to suggest: *Look, there's something wrong. I think I'm in danger.* However, I didn't want to look like a coward again. And that was another mistake. Gosh, I had made so many that day, I started to wonder if I really knew who I was.

When we got to the other side of the lake, there was some movement in the water. My phone's screen showed a Gyarados right in front of us. I shifted my eyes away from the phone to look at the commotion in the water, and I needed to rub my eyes over and over again to ensure my sight wasn't failing me. At that moment, I was absolutely sure that I was going crazy. Because there, in the middle of the lake, was a Gyarados – in the flesh. Nothing like bits and programming codes. It was standing there alive, before my very eyes.

Yup, it looked as if I had completely lost my mind.

## CHAPTER 3

# EVERYBODY HAS GONE CRAZY

I read somewhere that the power of logical thinking is unimaginable. Our brain is used to thinking rationally. So whenever something surreal happens, we instinctively try to find a compelling, rational explanation for it.

And that was exactly what I was doing while I gazed at the Gyarados. Perhaps it was the first sign of schizophrenia? Or some form of a passing hallucination? I was trying hard to put words together and say something that made sense.

'Um, guys? Are you seeing what I'm seeing?'

'There is a Gyarados right here!' shouted Cora. 'Let's get it!'

I don't know if you can understand the fear I felt. Perhaps it would help a little if you knew that the real Gyarados was gigantic, really huge actually, with fins and whiskers that made it appear even larger. It was far more frightening than the game version, believe me. And apparently, it was behind the whirlpool attack.

I took a deep breath. These were my best friends. They wouldn't think I was truly crazy, would they? We all joked around a lot, but this was serious. Something very weird was going on, and I was afraid, afraid of what the truth might be.

'Okay, I'm going to try to catch this cute one,' said Cora.

'Look, I don't think it's such a good idea...' I started to say.

'How come, Lucas? That's why we came here!' she added in disbelief.

'It's just that...' I began to explain, but it was too late. I was thrown backwards by a fierce jet of water and hurled some ten feet from where I'd been standing. It knocked the breath out of me. I was certain that it had been a hydro pump attack.

I started coughing and puking out all the water I had swallowed. 'I warned you!' I said with difficulty, standing up from the ground and still spitting out water.

'What was that?' asked Cora who, unlike me, was totally dry. If anything, this Gyarados was poking fun at me and no one else.

'Why did it attack me if you were the one who tried to catch it?' I asked while wringing out my T-shirt. Judging by the rate of these attacks, I wouldn't be dry anytime soon.

'Man, do you have a problem or something?' Samuel asked, walking over to me.

'This is serious, Samuel! It was the Gyarados who did this! He was there, right in front of us!'

'I know it was in front of us, you idiot. That's why I tried to catch it!' Cora shot back.

'No, I don't mean on my screen. It was *physically* here!'

'Hey, Samuel, your friend thinks Pokémon are real. How do we settle this?' shouted Cora, obviously pretending that I was out of earshot.

'Oh yeah, and this water jet was just my imagination, too, right?' I replied, now on the verge of losing my temper.

'It must have been some water pipe that burst or something. After all, this lake is artificial,' she concluded.

An interesting thing about human beings is that we believe only what we want to. It's useless to try to convince someone that something surreal has just happened. People see only what they want to see. And they'll accept any explanation that backs up their idea. Personally, I don't think this behaviour is quite logical.

Samuel moved closer to me, getting right in my face. 'Perhaps that falling tree bonked him on the head and we somehow missed it,' he replied. 'Perhaps if we bonk him on his head again, it'll help.'

'Ha, ha, ha, you are *so* funny! So where did the Gyarados go?' I wanted to know.

'I always knew that Lucas's fascination with Pokémon would drive him a little crazy.' Cora put her hand on my forehead, checking my temperature.

'Man, how strange. The app isn't detecting the Gyarados

anymore. Now it's only showing a bunch of Zubats nearby,' announced Samuel.

Everything was very bizarre, and I was starting to be afraid that I'd lost my mind for good. I wondered if I had played too much Pokémon and simply burned out my brain.

The city park was pretty large, with plenty of little ponds, gardens, lawns, and mainly pine trees. It was the perfect place to capture Pokémon of all kinds. But now I was thinking that we'd better get back to school.

'Oh, all right. Even if a Gyarados appeared, I don't think I'm on a high enough level anymore to catch it. What about heading back to school?' I asked.

'Lucas, we just have to keep on searching and we'll find more Pokémon. Stop the drama. You are really off-kilter today!' Cora put her hands on her hips and looked me up and down, analysing me.

'I really think I'm getting a little sick,' I said.

'You'll feel better once we start walking,' said Samuel as he sidled up beside me, placing a hand on my shoulder. I took my phone out of my pocket and opened the game app. Then an odd message from Professor Willow popped up:

Professor Willow: Hello, trainer. I am going to help you, but I need your help, too.

'Hey, guys. Take a look at this.' I showed them both the Professor's message on my phone's screen.

'Oh my, this is weird,' said Cora.

'I don't remember Professor Willow ever saying anything like this to me. Did your level go up?' asked Samuel.

'But what kind of help is he talking about? Did you do something different in the game?' asked Cora, snatching the phone out of my hands.

'No,' I explained. 'I just entered the app again and this sprang up. I didn't go up a level or anything like that.'

'Weird,' Samuel remarked.

While we walked along a path of pine trees, I tried to find something on the Internet about different messages coming from Professor Willow, but I couldn't find anything. Then, when it seemed like we were directly beneath the sun at 10:00 a.m., we heard a scream that stopped all of us in our tracks. Like I said, I don't understand why people choose to ignore the signs.

'And *now,* can we please go away?' I asked Cora.

'Shhh!' she said, raising an index finger to her lips. Samuel took some steps ahead, carefully, trying to be as quiet as possible.

'I can't see anything,' he whispered from somewhere in front of us.

'Let's go, Lucas,' Cora called out to me, taking me by the hand.

## CHAPTER 4

# WHAT THE EYES SEE, THE HEART FEELS... A LOT

If everything depended on me, we would have been in the science class, safe and sound. But it seemed that I had no influence in group decisions, especially not when the others openly doubted my mental stability.

We forged ahead but didn't hear anything else – which made me even more scared, because all of a sudden, the park fell into total silence and it started to feel very cold. The three of us walked together side by side. We put our arms around each other, trying to keep from trembling. I don't know if you have gone through a situation like this, where a huge open space, which is usually full of people, suddenly gets enveloped by a terrorising silence alongside a bone-aching coldness. I have to say, the only sounds I could hear were those of my heart beating faster and my teeth chattering.

'Look, I know you think I'm crazy and imagine things, but am I the only one who's freezing?' I asked, nudging closer to them.

'I swear that now *I'm* the one who's having trouble understanding anything,' said Cora, pulling me closer.

After walking for another few minutes without saying anything, we saw a man in a tracksuit, standing still and looking upwards. When we reached him, he was still staring into the sky.

'Hey?' Samuel said, touching the stranger's shoulder. The guy turned around with a frightened look on his face. 'Excuse me, but is everything all right?' Samuel asked.

'I...' the man started to say, before stopping and pointing upwards. We all looked up at the sky at the same time.

Snow was falling from the clouds, hitting the ground a few feet in front of us. When I realised it was snowing in the middle of spring, to my surprise my heart didn't beat faster. At that moment, it was as though it had stopped beating altogether. I felt Cora gripping my hand.

*What the heck was going on?*

'Okay.' Samuel started to speak again. 'Now *I* really think we should go back to school.'

'All right, I think we'd better go, too,' agreed Cora, and we all began to walk towards the nearest gate.

Everything was quiet still, but our walk towards the exit, with snow continuing to fall on our heads, caused us all to be more chilled to the bone than any of us had ever been before. We had to go around three pine trees that appeared to have just fallen on the ground. A part of the park's east section was destroyed, soaked in water, as though a high-pressure hose had been used to water the flowers and torn them to pieces. And off in the distance, a part of the garden looked to be completely ... frozen?

Steam was coming out of our noses and mouths as we breathed. Samuel couldn't stop shaking.

'I wonder if in this freezing cold, we could find an ice-type Pokémon?' he tried to joke.

'Seriously, Samuel, I don't think this is the time to even think about Pokémon...' As soon as Cora finished her sentence, we stopped in front of one of the bronze statues in the park that was totally encased in ice.

'What in the world did this?' fired Samuel, staring at the sculpture.

'Well, perhaps it's time we started running. How about that?' I suggested. 'I don't know what did this, but I don't want to stick around to find out!'

We looked at each other for a second and dashed off.

'Come on, guys!' Cora shouted, running off. 'Let's take this shortcut around the lake. We can take that bridge on the right!'

We went after her, and a moment later I was out of breath and lagging behind. Samuel was already halfway across the bridge while I had not even arrived at it. When Cora and Samuel reached the end of the lake's crossing, water started to gush up from the lake underneath it.

'Hurry up!' I heard Cora shouting to me. I ran as fast as I could.

'It's the Gyarados! It's the Gyarados again!' I shouted back. I managed to cross the bridge just after a violent jet of water shot upwards beneath it, snapping it in two.

'What the heck was that?!' shouted Samuel as we all heard the roar of water destroying wood. I felt my mobile vibrate in my pocket, and Cora's and Samuel's phones also started vibrating. Simultaneously, we checked our phones. A message from Professor Willow popped up in the app, saying:

Professor Willow: Here is my help.

The second we read the message, Cora's and Samuel's phones made a weird sound and their bodies shook violently for a few seconds, as though they were receiving an electric shock. I had no time to understand what was happening, because soon afterwards the Gyarados emerged again, this time by the edge of the lake. He had his mouth ajar, and as he turned to face us, he unleashed a fierce hydro pump that threatened to send us all flying.

'I think I'm crazier than Team Rocket blasting off at the speed of light,' muttered Samuel with his jaw dropping, seemingly petrified at the sight of the giant monster.

'Lucas! Samuel! Get out of there! Get away from the water!' shouted Cora, pushing Samuel and me violently to the right, behind a group of trees. With the sudden shove, her phone flew out of her hands.

'Ouch!' Samuel complained as he was crushed by the combined weight of Cora and me as we fell right on top of him. We stood up and Samuel examined his now-scratched elbows. 'Cora, please tell me that Lucas's illness has passed on to me, and that it's all an effect of the app's excessive light,' he begged as soon as he came to. Cora hid behind one of the trees, peering towards the lake.

'Samuel, if this is really the case, we are all going nuts for sure. Seriously, put your hand here and feel this. My heart is beating faster than ever before. I can't even breathe right,' said Cora, facing us again.

Samuel sat on a rock nearby and put his hands on his head. 'I think I'm having an anxiety attack,' he said as he started to pant, his eyes growing ever wider.

'But hey, wait a minute! Can you see the Gyarados? I mean, see it for real?' I asked, looking at both of them, waiting for their answers.

Cora, still near the trees, motioned me to come closer and, pointing toward the giant creature by the lake, said, 'You bet.'

One thing was quite clear to all of us: we were not safe here. The only thing we could do was run away.

'Okay, okay, let's calm down,' I started speaking. 'Samuel, take a deep breath, slowly, and let's get out of here!' I had already put my phone in my pocket. But it began vibrating again. I looked down at the new message:

Professor Willow: Now that I helped you with your friends, it's time you helped me.

'Uh, I still have to get my phone back,' Cora remembered.

This didn't sound good.

At all.

# CHAPTER 5

# THE WRONG PLACE AT THE WRONG TIME

Without wanting to sound pessimistic or anything like that, getting that message was not at all reassuring. I had a debt – to which I had not agreed upon in the first place – to a virtual entity, or whatever Professor Willow had become. You may think whatever you want, but I am sure the Professor does not keep sending weird messages directly to *you* or doing anything else of the sort.

I had already shown the message to Cora, and I had tried to show it to Samuel. But I was unsuccessful, as he insisted on saying that we had unwittingly eaten some sort of magic bean and were all 'daydreaming'.

'All right, all right,' said Cora, thinking aloud. 'I am going to run over there to get my phone, and you guys cover me, okay?'

'Are you crazy, Cora?' I almost shouted. 'I won't let you go back there!'

At this point, Samuel had finally stopped babbling senseless things to himself and was peering at his own phone.

'That's a Pokémon, right?' said Samuel, moving closer to me and Cora.

'That's the problem! Can't you see a very *alive* Gyarados over there?' I asked while I waved my arms incessantly, ready to dash away as fast as possible if I had to.

'Lucas, think with me a moment,' Samuel continued. 'If that is a real Pokémon that somehow escaped from the game, this means that we could possibly capture it with a Poké Ball from the game, couldn't we?' he enquired.

'Look, I don't know anymore what does and what doesn't make sense, so I say it's worth a try!' declared Cora, who went back to staring at the Gyarados again.

'But I don't understand why it is attacking us,' I added. 'It shouldn't be, since we weren't bothering it or anything. Did it feel threatened somehow?'

'But who said it wasn't disturbed, Lucas? We don't know exactly what's happening here,' pondered Cora.

'Perhaps Professor Willow can explain,' said Samuel as he aimed his mobile towards the Gyarados.

'No, Samuel. Don't waste a Poké Ball; we are too far away to be able to catch it.' I lowered my friend's phone and looked down at mine, scrolling through my list of captured Pokémon.

'Hey, guys. Since I can run faster than both of you, I can

go up there, capture the Gyarados, and get Cora's phone. Agreed?' said Samuel.

'Look, I don't think that running towards it is the best plan,' answered Cora. 'But if there isn't another way...'

Samuel prepared to run, while Cora and I watched from behind the trees. My heart was beating so fast that I was beginning to think that it would never resume its normal pace again.

Without notice, Samuel sped off toward the Gyarados. It soon noticed his approach and waved its fins continuously.

'Watch out! It's going to attack!' I shouted.

'And you think I don't know that?!' he replied in a panic as he grabbed Cora's phone off the ground. 'The time to do this is... NOW!' he screamed again, standing before the Pokémon and pointing his mobile directly at it. The water near them started to bubble and, looking from afar, I suddenly couldn't see the Gyarados anymore.

'Hey, it vanished!' Samuel shouted. 'It's gone!'

Having broken out in a cold sweat by now, I turned to Cora.

'This is not good,' she said.

Samuel didn't think twice before hurrying back in our direction. But as he got closer, trees along his path began tumbling over onto the ground, very close to his feet. It wouldn't be long before one of them hit him.

'Somebody please do something!' he shouted.

Cora and I looked at each other. Our hands were tied. How could we fight against a giant monster that had disappeared and was now somewhere else?

The Gyarados was destroying the park. I hoped that everyone around had noticed the danger and run away. I remembered the man admiring the snow. Would he be all right? The strength of the Gyarados's water attacks was astounding, I thought to myself. Whatever his problem was, he had to be very angry about something.

'Lucas! Samuel's going to die!' Cora screamed with all her might. One of the pine trees ahead of Samuel looked as if it would fall down at precisely the moment he passed by. That was when we knew there was nothing else we could do. Only a miracle could save my friend.

The tree tumbled down and we heard the most horrible cry of pain I've ever heard in my life. Cora and I quickly hurried closer.

'Somebody get me out of here! Ah!' Samuel shouted as Cora and I breathed deep sighs of relief when we saw he hadn't been killed. 'Help me out! What are you waiting for?!'

A part of the treetop had crashed into Samuel's arm, pinning him to the ground. He couldn't stand up. I kneeled down to look directly into his face.

'Are you okay?' I asked.

'Of course I'm not okay. My arm was just crushed by a tree. I'm not okay *at all!*' he yelled once again.

Water jets kept gushing out of the lake with full force, and one of the trees behind us was struck by one of them, making us all cry out. Quickly, we tried to lift the tree a little to release Samuel's arm, but it was too heavy for the two of us to budge it at all.

'Oh, what a treat...' Samuel said with some difficulty.

Amid the mess, Cora pulled me aside, and with our backs to our friend, who was still groaning on the ground in pain, she muttered, 'So do you have any ideas what to do? Because I don't have any!'

I sat back on the ground beside Samuel, put my hands over my ears, and began swinging my body. I wanted to go home, cry, and call my mother all at once.

'HELP! HELP! HELP!' I started to scream at the top of my voice.

'Lucas! Stop! Do not panic! You are scaring Samuel!'

'*Not* panic?' I asked. 'Cora, now is probably the best time to panic! This place is being destroyed, and with us still here, we're likely to be smashed along with it. And we're trapped, because we can't manage to get Samuel out of here without help!' I shouted even louder.

'OH MY, SAINT JUDE, SAVE ME!' Samuel began to shout in desperation. 'All right! Lucas, Cora – leave me here to die! Save yourselves!'

'Samuel, please shut up and let me think,' Cora replied.

The fact that we were in serious trouble was not news, but at least the Gyarados seemed to have forgotten about us. *Think, think, think, Lucas,* I repeated in my mind. *Do not panic!* I tried to calm myself down. The park was completely flooded, there was no sign of anybody else around here, and I didn't know how long we would last if we were attacked by another Pokémon.

Our situation was hopeless.

# CHAPTER 6

# THE ADVANTAGES OF HAVING A WORKING BRAIN

If in doubt, call the police.

This is a really good motto. I should remember it more often. After all, that's what I usually think about when I watch horror movies. Don't ask me why, but people never remember to call the police in scary movies.

'Cora, there's no other way. We should call the police!' I told my friend, barely containing my desperation.

'Police? Wouldn't it be better to call the firemen?' she replied.

I thought to myself and concluded that I didn't care exactly who she called, as long as she called soon, and that someone would be coming to rescue us before we were destroyed along with the rest of the park.

'It's all the same, Cora! All the same! Just call *somebody!*' I shouted, beginning to panic again.

While Cora picked her phone up off the ground and phoned the police, I checked the local news websites and Twitter for some information.

STRANGE ACCIDENTS ALL OVER
THE CITY. POLICE ADVISE RESIDENTS TO
STAY INDOORS
CLASSES SUSPENDED IN ALL SCHOOLS
CIVILIANS, WAIT FOR MORE INFORMATION

'IT'S THE END OF THE WORLD,'
*says local church priest*
CITY PARK TOTALLY DESTROYED
*Park users report seeing snowfall in spring*
ACCIDENTS STILL HAPPENING
WITHOUT APPARENT CAUSE; POLICE INVESTIGATING

HOURLY NEWS @hourlynews
'All of this was caused by aliens.'
Check out the interview with ufologist Mariano Pinheiro.

'Lucas?' called Cora. Then she shouted. 'LUCAS?!'

'Ouch!' I said, putting my hands over my ears. 'What's the matter?'

'All the lines are busy!' she answered. 'I call and call and call, but I always get a busy signal!'

'How come?' I asked nervously, already punching in

999 on my phone. It rang and rang, but all I got was a busy signal.

'Oh God—' I muttered.

'—What happened?' Cora cut in. 'Nothing but busy signals, right?'

'Yes, but this, too. There are twenty-five unanswered calls from my mother.'

Cora looked at my phone's screen and went pale.

*I'll be grounded for the rest of my life,* I thought.

'I'd be glad enough just to survive this, even if I do get grounded for the rest of my life,' Samuel said, reading my mind.

'Okay, okay, let's not completely lose it,' I said, looking around. Half the trees of the park had been destroyed, the entire place was virtually flooded, and there were no signs of any of the flowers in the formal gardens remaining. The statues were gone, and at the far end of the park near the south entrance, nothing had been left intact. I realised that to 'not completely lose it' would be quite a challenge.

'Lucas?' called Cora. 'Lucas! Look, if you're coming up with a solution, you'd better think fast,' she said, adding hysterically, 'because the Gyarados has just remembered that we exist!'

I looked up ahead, following the path of broken, fallen trees leading to the lake, where the Gyarados was facing us. I opened the game app in my phone and checked how many Great Balls and Ultra Balls I had left. My player level was very high, way above that of Cora and

Samuel. At this point, we had no idea what to do, and even though I kept trying not to think the absolute worst was about to happen, I couldn't stop thinking that, above everything else, I really didn't want to die. There were so many things I still wanted to do, so many things I wanted to experience...

Suddenly, I ran in the direction of the Gyarados. I ran like never before and I stopped about six feet away from the Pokémon. I pulled out my phone and pointed it directly at the creature.

'Come on, Gyarados!' I shouted. 'I don't know where you came from or why you're here, but a Gyarados in my collection wouldn't be the worst thing in the world!'

I could feel the adrenaline coursing through my veins, and my heart was beating faster than ever. I took a moment to perfect my aim and launched a Great Ball toward the Gyarados, who, when seen through my phone screen, didn't look nearly as scary as its real-life counterpart. Perhaps if I focused only on the image displayed on the screen, I wouldn't be so frightened.

My legs got weak the moment I noticed that my Great Ball shot had missed. I had failed in my attempt to capture the Gyarados. I could try again, but I was sure the lake monster wouldn't give me a second chance. Pokémon always hate it when people try to capture them.

'Lucas! Come back here! NOW!' Cora screamed from behind, her voice sounding increasingly desperate.

But there would be no time to retreat now. The Gyarados was about to attack.

31

'FOR A THOUSAND POKÉ BALLS!' shouted Samuel very loudly, as though the pain he'd felt had suddenly passed.

I turned back to face my friends, trying my best to ignore the fact that a Gyarados was about to kill me in the next couple of seconds. Then I noticed that a Bulbasaur was beside Cora. It was fairly small and looked friendly, perhaps because it was beside its trainer. In physical form, it didn't look frightening as the Gyarados did. The Bulbasaur looked happy.

'Bulbasaur, I am very glad that you exist and everything, but get Lucas out of there now!' ordered Cora. The Pokémon dashed towards me, grabbed me by the waist with its vines, and picked me up and deposited me safely behind it. Then it launched a leaf blade toward the water monster, who turned to retreat. I approached the lake for a second attack. This time, I was going to unleash an Ultra Ball.

'Go, Ultra Ball, help me!' I said to myself, launching the ball through the phone towards the Gyarados, who was now fleeing. The ball trembled, one, two, three times.

Moments like this, when I'm not sure if a ball attack I've used in the game was able to capture the targeted Pokémon or not, were too much for me. It's always too much anxiety, too much expectation, and, being a matter of life or death, too much stress. This was no time to marvel at Cora's Bulbasaur.

Then the ball stopped trembling. I had made it! I now had a very powerful, very dangerous Gyarados in my possession. I took a deep breath and looked at the Bulbasaur and my two friends behind me.

'Phew!' said Samuel.

It was time to catch my breath and find a safe way to get home.

# CHAPTER 7

# SOME UNEXPECTED SOLUTIONS

**P**erhaps it wasn't the best idea.

While I was admiring my Gyarados, I accidentally ended up accessing my Pokémon list and my Charmander's information. I couldn't help but wonder if my little monster would also come to life like Cora's Bulbasaur had done. Then, the second I touched its image on my phone's screen, my first Pokémon emerged in front of me, spitting out little flames in my direction. Hmmm, it looked like I'd chosen a temperamental guy as my first Pokémon.

'Ouch!' I shouted, grabbing my shoulder that had been charred by the Charmander's fire. 'Don't you know that I'm your trainer? Show a little respect!' I said to the little orange monster who had fire dancing on the end of its tail.

'In a little while, he'll calm down and get nicer,' Cora

said, coming closer and leaving Samuel alone on the ground. 'Bulbasaurs are usually friendly. But you still might have to get to know your Charmander a little better.'

'This is great, Cora, but I don't think we're going to have time for that,' I said, opening my phone's browser and showing her the headlines that had appeared in the newspapers and social media about strange happenings and all sorts of accidents.

'And are some people are saying it's … alien stuff?' she asked.

'That's nothing!' I answered her with a frown. 'Some people are saying it's the end of the world, and I wouldn't find it all that surprising if that turns out to be the truth.'

At the moment I said that, what seemed to be a giant bird passed above us in the sky. I hadn't got a clear look, and I wondered if I had seen what I suspected I had.

Cora continued reading the news headlines for a few minutes, and I kept admiring my Pokémon – from a safe distance, of course. This day was all surreal and scary, and it had left me scared to death. On the other hand, wasn't it wonderful to be there beside my Charmander, which was very much alive? I mean, seriously, it's practically a dragon! I always found it to be more of a dragon than a lizard since it spits fire and also has a flame on its tail. I somehow no longer cared about my burned shoulder. Or about the fact that the world seemed to be ending, with Pokémon destroying everything and whatnot.

'Hey, guys! Can somebody get me out of here?' Samuel shouted from under the treetop, one arm still stuck beneath it. 'I know that everything is super amazing with the Bulbasaur and the Charmander here with us, but I was really looking forward to living my next ninety years with two functional arms.'

Only then did Cora and I remember our friend, who was still caught under a broken treetop. His situation had not improved at all. His face was dirty and his clothes were soaked and full of leaves and small branches. The arm caught under the tree was starting to bleed a little, which began to worry me.

'Oh, Samuel! Wait – hang in there. We have a way to get you out,' said Cora as she walked over to Samuel. 'Bulbasaur, can you help our friend, please?'

Immediately the Bulbasaur swung into action, using its vines to lift the tree and throw it aside, releasing Samuel's arm from under all that weight.

'Thanks, Bulba.' Cora caressed the little grass Pokémon's head.

'Bubaa, bubaa,' responded the Pokémon.

'Ah, how cute!' Cora let out her sweet, little-girl voice, which she usually used when she was very excited.

'Now, Samuel, I don't think you should get up and start running around just yet. Let us take a look at you first,' I said to my friend.

'All right, I'll sit still. I don't even want to look at my crushed arm. I just wonder how much of it is left that I'll still be able to use,' Samuel added in a whimpering voice.

I reviewed the damage with Cora. Though it was far from a beautiful sight, it didn't appear to be beyond saving. I thought a good cast and healthy dose of painkillers might fix the situation.

'It's okay, Samuel,' I said, turning to face him. 'Much better than I thought.'

'Look,' instructed Cora, 'I'm going to support your arm, and you try to sit up very, very slowly, okay?'

The expression of dread on Samuel's face made me bite my lower lip. I really wouldn't want to be in his shoes. After all, it was a broken arm, and a broken arm must hurt something awful. Cora and I squatted down, and she cradled his hurt arm and tried to mirror Samuel's movements as he raised his body to sit up.

'Real slow.' I repeated Cora's words.

'OUCH! FOR THE LOVE OF POKÉMON! I THINK I'M GOING TO DIE OF PAIN!' Samuel screamed as Cora lifted his wounded arm. 'IT'S BROKEN, IT'S BROKEN! I AM SURE THERE IS NO WHOLE PIECE OF BONE IN THERE!'

'It's going to be all right, Samuel. Just take a deep breath,' Cora said, trying to calm him down while he finally sat up. Cora positioned Samuel's arm with his wrist at the same height as his belly button. 'Lucas, can you lend me your sweater? I am going to improvise a sling for our friend here.'

'My what? Hey, did you happen to notice it's still *snowing* over there?' I asked, reluctant to take off my only sweater.

'Boy, stop whimpering,' Cora shot back, 'or else I'll ask your Charmander to help you with your cold problem!'

I took off my sweater and handed it to her. Cora placed

the sweater underneath Samuel's broken arm, lifting the sleeves up and tying them tightly around his neck, so that his broken arm was quite secure against his body. We helped him stand up. His face was pale.

'Well, we need to go to the hospital now,' I announced.

'And more than likely it'll be a right mess over there,' Cora completed my thought.

'I hope those rogue Pokémon haven't killed all the doctors,' said Samuel, as though he were pleading to the heavens or something like that.

It's always good to keep a positive attitude.

# CHAPTER 8

# NOTHING IS SO BAD THAT IT CAN'T GET WORSE

**W**e didn't see any Pokémon along our walk to the park's exit apart from my Charmander, Cora's Bulbasaur, and Samuel's Squirtle, which had joined us.

Wherever we passed, however, there was only destruction. The place that we had known as the park would never be the same. The good news was that we didn't find any bodies, or injured people, or indeed anything of that sort. People must have left the place at the first signs of danger, something that my friends and I were apparently unable to do.

'Okay, it's time to go back into the Poké Ball, Bulbasaur,' Cora told her Pokémon, scratching the top of its toad head.

'Bulbasaur, bulba,' the little monster grumbled in a friendly tone.

Samuel's Squirtle was already back in its Poké Ball, or in the app, to be more precise. My Charmander, however, was the most stubborn creature of the three. I tried to recall it to its Poké Ball several times in an attempt to send it back to the app, but I failed. It spat fire, made grimacing faces, and slashed its tail about, looking furious.

'I give up,' I sighed, facing my Charmander. 'As luck would have it, I chose the most problematic Pokémon.'

'Look, you knew what you were getting into! We always knew that Charmanders were a little temperamental,' Samuel replied.

'Yes, but that was irrelevant to the game, because in it, the Pokémon do not display a personality! How could I know that they would turn into live beings?' I was starting to lose my temper.

'Well, in any case, I guess he'll have to keep walking with us,' said Cora, who was already leaving the park.

'Won't people be afraid?' I asked, running to catch up with Cora. Samuel was just behind us, with the Charmander following at the end of the line, walking as if he was being forced to do so.

'Uh, I don't think that's going to be a problem,' commented Samuel, gesturing around with his good arm.

The usually busy avenue was totally empty. There were no cars passing by, nor was there anybody to offer us help or explain what had happened. I was also ignoring my parents' calls, as were Cora and Samuel.

We couldn't possibly take a bus, simply because there weren't any on the streets. A few crashed cars were abandoned in the middle of intersections, some with wisps of smoke still emanating from them, and some buildings had been damaged. The scene was reminiscent of a post-apocalyptic horror film and it sent a shiver down our spines, which, when added to the silence all around us, gave a sensation of imminent danger.

We were on high alert because, as passionate game-players, we had actually planned many ways of surviving a zombie apocalypse if such a thing was to happen. Shockingly, the time to put those plans into practice had arrived.

Cora peered into her phone's screen, reading the news and checking social media, and I continued to follow the game app so as to prevent us from coming across any more Pokémon.

'Guys, according to the app, there is a Clefairy at the square!' I said, worried. 'What should we do?'

'Oh, I wonder if the real Clefairy is cuddly like in the drawing?' said Cora excitedly.

'We won't find it so cuddly if it starts attacking us!' I exclaimed. Jeez, was I the only one who was afraid and worried?

'You just have to be careful with it … and hope no one has bothered it,' Samuel said.

We headed to the square, but nobody was there. The area was so small that there wasn't any space for such a big Pokémon to stay hidden for long.

'Hmm…' Cora shrugged her shoulders.

Behind us, the Charmander coughed and a few embers

41

fell onto the concrete ground. Judging by its expression it was very distressed.

Using his good arm, Samuel took out his phone and opened the app. 'You two, I think you'll want to see this,' he announced. Cora and I got closer to look at the screen, on which we now saw a Clefairy. Samuel launched a Poké Ball to catch it.

'But how come…?' remarked Cora.

*How come indeed!* I thought to myself. Whenever I think I'm finally beginning to understand something, I always realise that, in fact, I understand nothing.

We stood there for a few minutes looking at each other's faces, not knowing what to say or do. Everything was so confusing. Nothing made sense. Without an answer, we resumed walking in the direction of the nearest hospital, this time without worrying too much about any Pokémon that popped up in the game app.

We entered the hospital, in company with the Charmander, but to our surprise, nobody seemed to have noticed the Pokémon.

So that's why there were so many reports of mysterious accidents, I realised. Nobody could see the Pokémon.

*Except us?*

Now that was pretty unbelievable!

Inside the hospital, chaos was everywhere. I think all the people in the city had congregated at the same place. Everywhere you looked, there were men and women in need of attention: injured, cut, burned – you name it. I sat on a chair, hoping we wouldn't have to wait too long to be attended to, while Cora and Samuel headed to the front desk and handed over Samuel's ID card so as to prove his identity.

'Where are the boy's parents?' asked the receptionist.

'Look, are you aware of what's happening in the city?' Cora nearly shouted. 'We have no clue where any of our parents are! The only thing I know is that a tree came crashing down on his arm, so he needs medical care!'

The woman faked a smile, then looked at Samuel's ID and wrote down his name. 'You can take a seat; he'll be attended to,' she said.

'Will it take long?' asked Samuel, growing pale with pain again.

'Since we have many patients in critical conditions, it may take a while ...a few hours,' she answered.

'A few hours?' He almost fainted.

Cora, who is the quickest-thinking person I know, got out her phone and called somebody.

'Hello? Uncle Sergio?' she spoke to the person she'd called. 'Do you happen to be in the hospital? I have a problem. Yeah, at the reception desk. Okay.' She hung up.

I stood up as soon as she ended the telephone conversation. Cora looked at us with a raised eyebrow using her I-can-fix-anything look, and Samuel and I shrugged.

'Problem solved,' she declared. 'Now we just need to figure out how to get home without being eaten alive by our parents.'

She had just finished saying this when my phone vibrated with a new message from Professor Willow.

'Guys, I don't think our parents are our biggest problem just yet,' I said.

We looked at each other after I showed them the screen. I could hear my Charmander making a noise that was close to laughter.

Professor Willow: Congratulations, Lucas. You are the Pokémon trainer with the highest level in your city.

Professor Willow: As you can see, things are out of control … If the gyms of the three original teams are conquered, it will all be over. We are counting on your help to return them to their legitimate leaders.

Professor Willow: Oh, and don't forget to save the world.

44

# CHAPTER 9

# I DIDN'T ASK TO BE BORN IN THE FIRST PLACE

t this point in my life, I had already been forced to do many things I didn't agree with. I had to go to school, do ridiculous amounts of homework, read boring books, make my bed, and take baths. I didn't want to be forced to save the world, too. It was too much responsibility. I didn't expect to have to take on a commitment of that level until at least my thirties.

Cora's uncle Sergio set Samuel's arm in a cast, and we finally phoned our parents. Then Uncle Sergio drove us home through the deserted streets. The Charmander, who had refused to go back to the Poké Ball, was with us in the car.

'Lucas! Are you okay?' shouted my mother as soon as I walked into the house. She hugged me and looked me up and down. 'What is this burn on your shoulder? Does it hurt?' she asked, lifting the sleeve of my shirt.

I tried to calm her down. 'It's nothing, Mum. Just a little burn. It's all right.'

After she released me from her suffocating hug, her expression shifted from one of relief to one of anger. 'You bunked off school, Lucas, in the middle of a disaster! And on top of that, you don't answer your phone!' Her shouting became louder and louder. 'DO YOU HAVE ANY IDEA HOW WORRIED WE WERE? WE THOUGHT SOMETHING TERRIBLE HAD HAPPENED TO YOU!'

I stood still and listened, waiting to go to my bedroom. While distracted by my mother, I didn't see the Charmander's tail brushing against the living room curtains, setting them ablaze. My mother hurried to put out the growing fire. I grabbed this opportunity to go to my bedroom, my ill-tempered Pokémon accompanying me.

From the living room, I heard my mother shout:

'You are forbidden to leave the house!'

My phone's battery was at three per cent. Huh! These people can lose control and create real Pokémon to destroy the real world, yet they can't make a game that doesn't consume all your battery power in a matter of hours. I plugged my phone into a wall socket and opened my messages:

*Samuel:* As predicted by my superpowers, I am grounded for the rest of my life.

*Cora:* Yeah, me too. But my whole family is, because it seems nobody can go out.

*Lucas:* I'm grounded, too. And the Charmander set the curtains on fire.

*Cora:* Really?? LOL.

*Samuel:* So how are we going to escape and go out?

*Lucas:* Go out??? Are you crazy???

*Cora:* COME ON, LUCAS!! HOW ARE WE GOING TO SAVE THE WORLD BY STAYING INDOORS?!

*Lucas:* I don't know, can't we just call Superman?

*Samuel:* No way, pal. You have no choice. YOU ARE THE CHOSEN ONE. You are practically Harry Potter.

Samuel had to stop this train of thought, I reasoned to myself. I couldn't save the world—I was just a kid. And I hadn't even succeeded in making friends with my Pokémon in the first place, which should have been a basic task for a superhero.

*Lucas:* Drop it, my bed feels wonderful. At least the part the Charmander hasn't charred yet.

*Samuel:* This is serious, guys. I searched the forums and discovered that a gym was mysteriously conquered by an unknown team.

*Cora:* Unknown team? What do you mean???

*Lucas:* There are only the Valor, the Mystic, and the Instinct.

*Samuel:* That's what's odd. This team is named Conquer. And their gyms are black.

*Lucas:* How crazy.

*Cora:* How creepy.

*Lucas:* I wonder if this has to do with the Pokémon destroying everything...

*Samuel:* I think this is quite clear. If Professor Willow has asked you to retake the gyms...

*Cora:* Yes, I think it's obvious he's talking about this team that did not exist in the game until just yesterday!

*Lucas:* It may well be the case, but he'll have to find someone else to save the world, because I have no talent for this.

*Cora:* Lucas, I hate to say it, but you are the best Pokémon player I've ever known.

*Samuel:* I agree with Cora.

So there it was, I had no choice. I would do this because of pressure from a virtual entity and those who claimed to be my best friends. Cora and Samuel devised a plan in which I would strategically sneak out of my home at night without anybody in my family noticing. Then I had to ride my bicycle in the dark, alone, through the deserted streets to Cora's house, which wasn't far from where Samuel lived. It goes without saying that I was not particularly thrilled at all with the plan.

I loaded a backpack with everything I was going to need: a powerful torch, water, chocolate, a first-aid kit, a portable mobile phone charger, and charging leads. At eleven o'clock, when I was sure everyone was asleep – they had all nodded off quickly because they were tired and stressed out – I carefully sneaked into the living room.

'Watch your step, Charmander,' I warned my new friend. This Pokémon was very clumsy, and I was hoping he wouldn't set anything else on fire.

'Charmander! Charmander!' he answered sulkily, and I rolled my eyes.

The only relief from darkness in the house was the downstairs hall light, but the Charmander was helping to illuminate our way with its tail. I was afraid of the noise my trainers would make as I stepped on the linoleum floor. When I got to the living room, I was startled by a noise from the window. The Charmander assumed its attack position, as though it expected something was going to approach it.

'It's all right,' I said to it, in an attempt to calm both of us down.

A similar noise came from the front door, as if it was being shaken by someone very strong. I held my breath and the light in the corridor began to blink, which made me even more scared.

I looked all around me, expecting something else to happen, until my phone vibrated in my pocket. There was a message in the game app. It said:

Last Master: It looks like we are together in this battle.

# CHAPTER 10

# GRAB ALL YOU CAN AND RUN!

Cycling alone on deserted streets at night made me long for my bed. The atmosphere was so sinister that I finally convinced the Charmander to go back inside the Poké Ball. Now that it was pretty quiet, both on my phone's screen and in the outside world, I was even more scared. That message from the Last Master repeated endlessly in my head.

The only sound I could hear was that of my bike as I pedalled along past the five blocks of flats up to Cora's home. The cold was particularly brutal at that time of night. I looked up at the sky and saw a giant blue bird pass very close to the building rooftops. I braked as soon as I saw it, because I was sure that it was a legendary Pokémon: the powerful Articuno.

After digesting that image, I pedalled like crazy to pass

the next two road intersections, when I saw Cora and Samuel, both wearing thick coats, waiting for me on the dark street with Cora's bike sitting between them.

'Hey, what's the hurry?' asked Cora as I got off the bike.

'This city is sinister,' I answered, catching my breath. 'And very cold.'

'Indeed,' agreed Samuel. 'I want to know if this freezing temperature is a Pokémon thing.'

'Funny you should say that...' I started saying, a little awkwardly, '...but I think I saw an Articuno on my way here.' I swallowed my words a bit, because that legendary Pokémon was next to impossible to capture. If the world depended on it getting caught, then we might as well just give up now.

Cora and Samuel looked at me with no discernible expression on their faces, as though they had not quite understood what I had said. Then Cora raised an eyebrow and looked directly into my eyes.

'An *Articuno?* A legendary Pokémon ... here ... in town?' she asked incredulously.

After all we had gone through that day, I would have been quite upset if they'd doubted anything I'd said I had seen. At this point, I didn't doubt anything anymore.

'I'm serious, Cora! It was an Articuno, really! I think I had already seen it down at the park earlier.'

'Look, it makes sense,' Samuel considered. 'All this cold could be the Pokémon's fault, and so could the snow we saw at the park!'

Samuel was right. The Articuno must have been behind all of that. Which put us in a very bad position.

'Well, this is not good,' he pondered. 'Not good at all.'

'None of the legendary birds has appeared in the game so far. This is quite an event. Especially if the other two birds are around as well,' I said, picking my bicycle up off the ground.

'Yeah, and if they are, we are going to have three times the trouble!' joked Samuel, peering into his phone.

'Either way, we've got to proceed with the plan,' Cora reasoned. She tried to call our attention to what was at stake. 'The nearest black gym is at the church. But first, we need some other things.' She looked at us with a half-smile.

'Am I the only one who hates it when she makes that face?' I asked Samuel.

'Not at all.' He rolled his eyes.

I sat down on the kerb, trying to put my thoughts in order. According to Cora's plan, it was time for 'refuelling'. I was afraid to ask what she meant by that.

'Lucas, get on your bike. Samuel, come with me!' Before Samuel could jump on behind her, Cora had her feet on the pedals.

I got on my bike and began pedalling hard to keep up with them.

'Where are we going?' I called out to my friends.

'There is a high concentration of PokeStops downtown. We need to refuel for the battles,' explained Samuel.

'We have to gather as many Poké Balls and potions as possible,' added Cora, as our bikes climbed the hill.

We headed downtown via a shortcut. 'Do you really

think I can take these gyms back and beat this guy?' I asked them. (Even though I had already decided that someone like me would never be able to do something as great as this.)

'Lucas, you are level thirty-seven!' Cora exclaimed, struggling to pedal while carrying both her own weight and Samuel's.

'I did some research! There are only two people with the same level as you!' Samuel added, holding on to Cora's waist with his one good arm. 'And no one is above yours!'

I liked that information. It meant that I was one of the best players. I felt a spark of – dare I say it? – hope.

After riding down the hill, we stopped in front of the bookshop, the first PokeStop we would visit.

'Nice work, guys. See how many potions, revives, and Poké Balls you can get here,' Cora ordered, climbing off her bicycle and carefully helping Samuel get to his feet.

'And, Lucas, I think that aside from refuelling, you should capture as many Pokémon as possible, even if they're ones you have already, to win experience,' advised Samuel as I got off my bike. I was already checking how many things I could take at the PokeStop and which Pokémon might be around.

I found a few Great Balls and a few Ultra Balls in the shop, but I hadn't managed to win any Master Balls. I also had a considerable number of common Poké Balls, eggs, and potions. All of this could be useful down the road, so we grabbed what we could at that PokeStop.

We rode around for almost an hour, stopping at every

PokeStop for refuelling. I captured more Pokémon, even some new ones, thus increasing my count. I was on my way to becoming a Pokémon Master!

'Are you getting any stardust?' asked Samuel.

'And are you sending your repeat Pokémon to Professor Willow to gain candy?' Cora inquired.

I shot them an angry look, somewhat unintentionally, but my dismay was quite obvious. Were they trying to teach me how to play the game? I was doing everything I could think of to increase my player level and my Pokémon level, but the game was becoming increasingly hard and more stressful every time I went up a level. They didn't have to remind me to do all those things. After all, they had said I was one of the best players!

## CHAPTER 11

# I ALWAYS HATED HORROR MOVIES

I thought we had done everything possible to increase our chances of defeating this mysterious fourth team. Cora and Samuel were on a reasonable level, and they had plenty of Pokémon and potions in their arsenal.

After catching what we could at the last PokeStop, Cora got on her bicycle, ready to set off.

'So shall we go? Are you guys prepared?' she asked.

I looked at Samuel and we said nothing. We were not prepared at all, but it seemed that out of our limited options, we were the best of the lot. I climbed on my bike, Samuel got on the back, and we were ready for a thirty-minute ride to the gym.

Along the way, the cold got even worse. Our breathing formed clouds of steam, and our bodies quivered.

'If I don't get killed by an aggressive Pokémon, I will certainly die of cold,' said Samuel.

I was still not used to the complete emptiness into which the city had been transformed. It was nothing like it had been before, what with the crisp sun, things happening everywhere, bars and squares full of people well into the evening ... Nothing of that life seemed to exist anymore. And I couldn't believe that all of this had been caused by Pokémon, the thing I loved most in life. (I mean, after my family, my friends, and that kind of thing.)

We got to the church as the cold was reaching a glacial level. It was impossible to stand still, so we kept bouncing on our feet while still astride the bikes. The lights were completely out in the block of flats, and there was no movement anywhere near the church.

'Good,' said Cora. 'Here we are.'

'Yes, here we are, on the verge of freezing to death,' said Samuel as he slowly got off the back of my bicycle.

I climbed off next, grabbed my phone, and took a long look at the black gym on the screen. I tried to touch it, as we normally do in the game, but nothing happened.

'Hmm, you two?' I tried to get their attention, as they were now more concerned with getting warm than with our mission.

'What's the matter?' asked Cora, hugging me.

'Nothing happens in the app when I touch the gym,' I explained.

She began to speak: 'Which means that—'

'—we will have to enter the gym "for real",' Sam interrupted, cutting her off.

I stopped peering into the phone and faced the church. There wasn't a single light on in there, at least none that would allow us to see through the windows and stained glass. As you may know, in the game it's not necessary to enter a gym to fight against the Pokémon that protects it and conquer it for your team. The player can battle from the outside – he simply needs to be close enough to engage.

When I agreed to our plan to fight for the gyms, I didn't take into account that it would be quite different from the game. I knew that I had captured a real Gyarados, and that I also had a temperamental Charmander at my disposal. I also knew as well that, if I wished, I could bring all my virtually captured Pokémon into the real world. But sometimes reality hits me head-on in an odd way. I didn't feel prepared for this.

'Hey, Lucas!' Samuel called to me. 'Let your Charmander come back to us, please.'

'Why? I don't think he'd obey me if we needed his help. You'd be better off releasing the Bulbasaur and the Squirtle.'

'Lucas, stop whimpering and unleash the little dragon – we need it!' he insisted.

'Okay, but don't tell me later that I didn't warn you,' I threatened, opening the Poké Ball and releasing the Charmander, which was quite unhappy at having to return.

'Done!' Samuel shouted triumphantly. 'Now we have a source of light *and* heat.'

How come I didn't think of that? My friend was indeed a clever guy, I had to admit.

'Good idea, Samuel. But why you didn't release one of your fire Pokémon?' I asked him.

Samuel wagged his finger at me. 'That would have been risky. What if one of them got out of control?'

He was absolutely right. If my Charmander was apt to be destructive, imagine what an upset Charizard or an Arcanine could do?

'Okay, but can we go inside now? Or should we stay here until the world ends?' said Cora impatiently, already releasing her Bulbasaur and approaching the church's entrance. Using both her hands, she turned the big iron doorknob. We heard a low-pitched click.

It was just like a horror movie.

## CHAPTER 12

# DON'T PUT YOUR FUTURE IN THE HANDS OF A CHILD

These spikes of adrenaline were really starting to get to me. As we entered the church, my stomach felt as if I had eaten three tons of rotten food.

The church's main hall had almost no benches, and any altar images there might have been had been removed. The only sources of light present were the Charmander, the torches we had brought, and the screens of our phones, which were always ready to go.

We were three kids with three Pokémon inside a freezing, partially destroyed, eighteenth-century building. Our teeth chattered non-stop, and Samuel was practically hugging the Charmander in an attempt to warm himself up. Icicles of frost covered what was left of the wooden church benches like motes of dust. Apart from that, there was no sign that anyone was there, not even a single noise.

Cora pointed her torch beam upwards, above the altar, revealing the sign of the Mystic team, an Articuno. But scrawled over it was black graffiti depicting a Mewtwo. A shiver came over me when I saw that.

'Hey, guys?' I said, swallowing my words. 'I might have forgotten to mention something important...' I said, and then swallowed my words.

All five of them – my two friends and the three Pokémon – looked at me immediately.

'The Last Master sent a message,' I informed them.

'The Last Master?' asked Samuel. 'What's wrong with you? Did you drink some stardust tea?'

'Look, I'm not sure, but that's his name, or his avatar. I don't know.'

'What did he say?' asked Cora, her eyes wide open.

'That "It looks like we are together in this battle",' I told them, using my torch to illuminate the graffiti above the altar again.

Deep in thought, we all remained silent. With each passing minute, things got more serious. I heard Cora sigh deeply.

'Did Professor Willow get in touch again?' she asked.

'No, I haven't heard from him since we left the hospital,' I answered, discouraged.

'This Willow has not been a good mentor, has he?' remarked Samuel.

The silence was so deep that our voices echoed around the church's nave, sounding much more powerful than they really were. Suddenly, Cora's Bulbasaur began to quiver, as though the cold had increased tenfold. Seconds later, an ice-cold breeze washed over us, drawing us even closer to the Charmander, who, at this point, was sulking more than he ever had before.

'Well, since there's nobody here, I think we can go, right?' I asked.

'Take it easy, Lucas. We've got to check everything out,' Samuel said, walking towards the altar.

Making a hissing noise, a Ninetales, accompanied with an icy breeze, passed quickly through the church before heading to the back and vanishing into thin air. The three of us looked at each other, spooked.

'At least it didn't stay for the party,' Samuel said.

'We need clues, otherwise the world is in serious trouble,' said Cora. 'Churches always have those little rooms where the priests stay, don't they?'

I sighed. I didn't know how I happened to be friends with them, me being such a scaredy-cat.

'Hey, Lucas. You are aware that the Chosen One here is you, right?' reminded Samuel with a laugh.

'I don't know how you can joke at a time like this,' I said. I went on walking behind Cora, with Samuel in the lead.

I was sort of losing my temper with them. The Charmander didn't help, given that it was glued to Cora's side and seemed to like her better than me, his own trainer.

When we got closer to the altar, all our torches went out at the same time, which stopped us dead in our tracks. We listened, waited, and held our breath.

'All right, let's stay calm,' said Cora. 'We still have our Pokémon and our phones. Is everybody okay?'

'All clear,' Samuel replied.

'Buba,' said the Bulbasaur.

The Squirtle grunted in assent.

The Charmander spat out a little fireball in Cora's direction. She smiled and stroked its head.

'Lucas?' Cora and Samuel asked at the same time.

I was motionless, pretty sure that my heart had stopped beating and would not be returning to normal any time soon. With a hand on my chest, I tried to breathe in deeply, slowly, struggling not to give in to the urge to run away, screaming like a deranged person.

'Lucas?!' they called me again.

I came to, trying to suppress a panic attack.

'I'm fine, I'm fine,' I answered.

They both looked at me in the dim light, then resumed walking. I turned on my phone's torch.

'I'll lead the way with the Charmander,' declared Cora. 'You guys follow me.'

'Hey, wait a second here. You're a girl, so you've got to follow me,' objected Samuel. 'You know, for your own safety.'

Cora smiled. 'Look, Samuel. Don't get me wrong, but if I depended on you for my safety, I would've been dead a long time ago.'

'Buba!', Bulbasaur agreed.

I chose not to comment, since Cora was completely right. In a zombie apocalypse, she would most likely be the only survivor out of us three. If the whole world went that crazy, which now seemed quite likely, I'd be dead. And I wouldn't be the least bit surprised. I really mean it. Who in their right mind would put mankind's future in the hands of a kid like me? Surely, Professor Willow was not right in the head.

With the Charmander lighting the way, we followed behind Cora, pointing our phone beams in all directions. Our path led into a wooden hallway, which was also enveloped in total blackness. 'Whoever is here does not want any lights on,' Samuel commented.

Samuel's words made me shiver even more. With that cold still gripping me, I thought to myself that should I indeed survive the night, I would head right back home and fetch two more coats and a blanket to wear. Then I'd prepare myself for what was to come next.

# CHAPTER 13

# THESE ARE HARD TIMES FOR GAMERS

**W**alking in silent darkness had just been added to my list of the things I least liked to do. Any sudden sound would have shaken me to the core.

We continued behind Cora and came to a corridor with wooden walls and a floor that creaked with our every step. It was hard to keep our nerves under control, and even Samuel seemed to be scared. Of course, that shared fright only increased as the floor began to shake, as though it was trying to expel us from the hallway.

'Hang on!' Cora cried out, leaning on a wall for support. The Bulbasaur used its vines to stabilise itself, while the other two Pokémon were thrown about from side to side, unable to hang on to anything.

'I won't be able to hold on for long!' I shouted beside the Charmander, who was being knocked back and forth between both sides of the corridor. It was getting hurt and I couldn't do anything to help. It was like an earthquake; we were in serious trouble.

'Which Pokémon is doing this?' Samuel yelled. 'Can anyone see anything?'

'No!' shouted Cora. 'I dropped my mobile!'

'THERE IS A MAROWAK AT THE END OF THE CORRIDOR!' I yelled at the top of my voice. The Marowak was a little but strong, *very* strong, Pokémon.

'I can't see anything!' Cora replied.

Samuel shouted from behind, 'I think it's passing!' And then everything stabilised, and it was as though nothing had happened.

Our Pokémon fell down on the floor, worn out and hurt. I ran to the side of my Charmander, which had bruises on both sides of its body.

'I am so sorry, Charmander. Are you okay?' I asked. It didn't answer. It could only give me a tired look. I turned back and saw the Squirtle was injured, too. There was no trace of the Marowak anywhere.

I took my phone out of my pocket and placed my Pokémon back in the Poké Ball. I accessed my items and gave it a potion to restore its Hit Points (also known as HP).

Next, I accessed my Pokémon collection and touched the Charmander's image on the screen for it to come back to being with us, in real life.

'Yes! You're okay!' I said to it when I saw the potion had really worked. It looked at me and wagged its tail, slowly. Samuel did the same with the Squirtle, and Cora with her Bulbasaur, and then we were all complete again, ready to continue. If only there were potions and remedies for humans, too, I wished.

Cora grabbed her phone and adjusted her ponytail, which had come undone with all the shaking. 'We have to keep going,' she announced. 'I can see a door at the end of the corridor.'

We walked with slow and insecure steps, trying to postpone our arrival at that door as long as possible. Nobody wanted to meet the Last Master, not for real. Cora acted tough, but I knew she was just as afraid as the rest of us.

I once read somewhere that there are no such things as fearless and fearful people. The point is, we are all fearful. What distinguishes us is the way we respond to threats. Of course, everyone's heart beats faster when we are faced with fear; it's just that some of us do not let ourselves become too affected by such things. I am not one of these people – though you already knew that, didn't you?

We stood in front of the door and breathed deeply. My Charmander let out an unintelligible sound. Little by little, he was becoming more friendly. Cora looked both Samuel and me in the eyes. Then she turned and faced the door.

Cora slowly turned the doorknob. When she opened the door, a cloud of Zubats flew in our direction, cutting through the air at such high speeds that I was surprised they didn't slash into our skin.

'Watch out! They bite!' I warned. A bite attack is typical of these bats, which have the capacity to spread disease and destroy like a plague. One of them came at me, baring its sharp claws. I was steadying myself for the pain when the Charmander blasted the group of Zubats with its flamethrower, scattering them. They quickly flew away with charred wings.

Once we were all in the room, Cora shut the door, and we could finally breathe again. 'That was a close one!' she said.

'Thank you, Charmander.' I stroked my Pokémon's head.

'Thanks, indeed!' Samuel agreed, sitting down on the floor to rest.

'I hate Zubats,' I declared, and everyone agreed.

We illuminated the room, which looked like a rubbish tip. It was full of knick-knacks: chandeliers, candle boxes, cushions, wooden benches, books and bottles. There were religious pictures heaped in a corner. However, the items didn't appear to be dusty. They looked as if they had been put there fairly recently.

'I think someone made a "clean sweep" of the church and dumped everything in here,' remarked Samuel as he stood and picked up one of the pictures from the pile. 'I came to this church once, and many of these things were hung up in the nave. Some were even above the altar.'

'I think the Last Master wanted an empty place to do battle,' said Cora, observing the room.

I took one step towards a heap of wooden benches when we heard a noise coming from underneath. Scared, I let out a yell.

'What was that?' I asked, already backing away.

Cora walked closer to the Charmander, who was now lighting candles in a candlestick.

'Beware,' Samuel said to Cora, who, with the Charmander, was inching closer to the benches, lighting up the heap of wood. 'There may be more Zubats.'

Something darted away, as though it was trying to hide. There was tension in the air as even our Pokémon looked nervous. The Charmander assumed an attack stance.

'Leave me alone!'

We heard a female voice coming from beneath the pile.

'GO AWAY!' she screamed this time.

Cora looked at Samuel and me with an inquisitive expression.

'Who's in there?' Samuel asked.

'Just leave me be, and get out of here while you can!' she cried out. 'And thanks for getting rid of those Zubats. Irritating Pokémon!'

Cora moved ever closer, stooped, and peered into the gaps, trying to see who was in there.

'Hey, it's all right,' Cora said with a soft, kind voice. 'We won't hurt you.'

'It's not you I am afraid of, idiot,' the voice retaliated. 'If you're smart, you'll get out of here as fast as possible.'

'So what *are* you afraid of?' challenged Samuel, also getting closer.

'He said he'd be back,' said the girl. 'But I won't let him find me.'

'WHO?' shouted Cora, beginning to lose her temper.

'You wouldn't understand,' the voice answered.

Cora let out a long sigh, clearly irritated by the stranger's vague words.

'Bulbasaur, help me out here,' Cora asked, and the two of them began to remove the piled-up benches, searching for the owner of the terrorised voice.

'Stop!' shouted the voice. 'What are you doing? Get out of here!'

'We won't go away until you explain who you are and why you are hiding,' Cora said, while she continued removing the benches. Soon enough we could see a small girl hugging her knees. She had wounds and bruises all over her body.

'You don't understand,' she muttered, crying. 'You need to get out of here. You are too young…'

Though the girl appeared to be seventeen or eighteen – much older than we were – her body was shrunken down like that of a child. Her hair was long and so blonde that it looked nearly white.

'Can you tell me your name?' I asked, squatting in front of her.

'Blanche,' she answered.

My friends and I looked at each other.

How was that possible?

# CHAPTER 14

# WHEN TWO WORLDS MEET, YOU'D BETTER RUN

**W**e stayed in silence for a while, trying to digest the situation. Blanche was there before us, injured, scared, defeated. She was strong, I'd thought, invincible even. How could she be this way now? Scared to the point of being frightened of her own shadow?

Blanche was the leader of the Mystic team, and, like our Pokémon, she was in the physical realm now, in the flesh, and wearing a tattered blue uniform. It was evident that she had been in battle, though I was afraid to ask her exactly what had happened. I wanted to get out of there quickly and quietly, hoping that no one would notice my absence. Perhaps Cora could restore Blanche to her former glory by increasing her level as a player? She was, in all certainty, a better choice than me to lead us against the Last Master. What I really wanted to do was lie down in a foetal position and cry myself to sleep. If it really could get me out of this dreadful situation I was in, I would certainly do it.

'It's all right, Blanche.' Samuel edged closer to talk to her. 'I'm part of your team,' he said.

'Mystic is not my team anymore,' she replied, with fresh tears rolling down her dirty face.

Samuel faced her. At that moment, he didn't look like a ten-year-old boy anymore. He looked bigger, older.

'Blanche, you have to tell us what happened,' Cora insisted. 'If we don't know what or who we're dealing with, we'll get wiped out.'

'I am very sorry,' Blanche said, rubbing her hands across her face in an attempt to dry her tears, 'but you don't have the slightest chance.' Her expression was serious and devoid of hope. She had given up.

I sat down beside her on the floor because I was afraid of falling down, since my legs couldn't bear my weight any longer. I had the feeling that I was living out my final hours and I should run back and hug my parents, eat a whole tub of strawberry ice cream, and do my best to leave this place in peace, as it was almost certain that we weren't going to get through this alive.

My friends looked at each other, and the Charmander sidled up to me, warming up my body in the cold room.

'Why does the Mystic team not exist anymore?' asked Samuel.

'He did something when he brought us all here,' Blanche began to explain. 'He stole all of my Pokémon. He took away my Articuno! He is doing terrible things! He is scaring helpless Pokémon everywhere.' She started to cry again, and covered her face in shame.

'Is the Articuno really here?' I asked.

'Yes,' she sighed.

Cora put her hand on Blanche's shoulder. 'We're going to get your Articuno back,' she told the stricken woman.

The former awe-inspiring leader started laughing hysterically, as though Cora had told a great joke.

'Don't be silly, girl,' she said.

Cora became upset and quickly got on her feet.

'Okay, let's get out of here,' she said. 'We have to go after this Last Master.'

'You are incredibly naïve if you think you can beat someone like him,' Blanche replied, still sitting on the floor, surrounded by scattered wooden benches.

'Either we try, or we'll have to hide away like you,' Cora said to her as she turned to leave.

I stood up, but only because I didn't know what else to do. Samuel also motioned us towards the door.

'Let's go, Charmander,' I said to my Pokémon.

'He is controlling *everything*. If he gets the other two legendary birds, there will be no escaping,' Blanche said as she watched us prepare to leave.

We turned to face her, in silence. There was nothing more to say. We continued on our way and walked quietly up to the end of the corridor, coming to a spiral staircase. The first step to defeat the enemy was to find him, but we hadn't succeeded in that yet.

We climbed the stairs carefully in the dim half-light. This time, Samuel led the charge, followed by me, Cora, and then our Pokémon, who had enormous difficulty with the steps. Once again, the Bulbasaur's vines gave it an advantage in locomotion. Ever since it had helped us in the park, I was trying to understand why Bulbasaurs were initially so disdained as Pokémon by so many trainers. After all, they had skills that translated well beyond the battleground.

Samuel reached the top of the stairs. 'Guys, I think you'll want to see this,' he said.

Cora and I quickened our pace, nearly crashing into Samuel, who stood still on the top stair. The spiral staircase led into some sort of attic. Off to the right side, there was another staircase, which climbed higher and appeared to lead to the top of the church tower, where the bell was.

In the middle of the attic, a symbol of the gym – appearing the same as it did in the game app – was shining there hanging in mid-air, slightly illuminating the wooden floor like a hologram.

'Well, I think it's up to you now, Lucas,' said Cora, looking at me.

I swallowed hard and approached the hologram. A thousand things were going through my mind at that moment, but the most important one was deciding which Pokémon I would choose to defeat whatever it was that was defending the gym.

I grabbed my smartphone and touched the gym icon on the screen. Instantaneously, a Blastoise materialised in the room, facing us in an intimidating manner. Look, I don't know how you might feel if you were facing a Pokémon that intimidating, but I didn't feel good at all. The cannons protruding out of its shell were hissing, seemingly ready for combat. I think I was motionless for too long, because Cora and Samuel, fearing something awful, started shouting my name non-stop. It was too much for me to take for one night.

'Lucas! What's your strategy?' Samuel asked.

I kept on thinking. No choice seemed good enough. A powerful Pokémon like the Blastoise... what would be capable of beating a water monster like that?

My options were limited. And the best choice I reckoned I had was not among my favourite ones.

'What are you waiting for?' Cora asked, almost shouting.

The Blastoise didn't signal that it was going to attack, not before I started the battle. But my time had apparently come.

## CHAPTER 15

# A BLASTOISE IS A DIFFICULT CREATURE

I was never fond of the Grass-type Pokémon. I have nothing against them, if this happens to be your preferred type, but I could never work out how to use them correctly in fights in any of the Pokémon games I have played. So it was a tense moment for me when I chose an Exeggutor to go up against the giant Blastoise.

I can't say I was particularly confident in my choice, but I had to do what I thought was necessary. Grass-type attacks are very effective against Water-type Pokémon, which gave me an advantage. And luckily, I had captured an Exeggutor that already had a very high level. Then I spent my stardust, making it even stronger.

'I'm going with my Exeggutor,' I told Cora and Samuel. I put the Charmander into the Poké Ball and asked both of them to do the same with their Pokémon.

'A Grass-type may be a good choice,' Samuel agreed, positioning himself by my side.

'So get on with it!' shouted Cora, anxiously. 'What other type of Pokémon is good against the Water types?'

'Electric types usually work well,' I replied.

I looked ahead and faced the Blastoise again. It was snorting air through its nostrils, just waiting for my first move. It was no longer cold in the room, and my back began to sweat.

I grabbed the phone and scrolled through my Pokémon collection.

'Exeggutor, I choose you,' I said half-heartedly.

I touched the image of my Pokémon, and it appeared in real life in front of me, with its heads that resembled coconuts and a body that looked like a palm tree. I never tired of marvelling at each flesh-and-blood Pokémon that suddenly appeared before me.

As soon as it saw the Exeggutor arrive, the Blastoise started to move, its expression changing to one of sheer concentration, as it prepared an attack.

'Okay, Exeggutor,' I said. 'Time to use your Seed Bomb!'

My Exeggutor launched a powerful barrage of seeds toward the Blastoise, and they exploded as soon as they reached it, lighting up the room like fireworks. We covered our eyes immediately.

'My goodness!' Cora screamed.

Though the attack was impressive, it hardly affected the Blastoise. Now, taking its turn to attack, the Blastoise used Flash Cannon – an extremely strong Steel-type move – on the Exeggutor, which knocked it down and blinded us again. I have to say that battling in the game is nothing like battling in real life. The adrenaline overload I was feeling was so intense that I was surprised I hadn't run away yet. The Exeggutor stood up. I saw through the screen on my phone that its HP bar was much smaller. It was losing power.

'You're doing great, Exeggutor!' I said, trying to encourage it. From the window of the room, I saw the Articuno once again, passing with its majestic flight, going who knew where. I shifted my attention back to the battle. 'Guys, what should I do?' I shouted. 'The Exeggutor's strongest Grass-type attack is Seed Bomb!'

'Try again, Lucas!' Cora answered. 'I don't think any of its other attacks would even scratch that Blastoise!'

I thought that if I shouted the attack, the Exeggutor would unleash a more powerful one, so I shouted 'SEED BOMB!' as loud as I could. But the damage that was inflicted upon the enemy wasn't as serious as I'd hoped for. I took a deep breath and sighed. Cora and Samuel stared at me.

Next, the Blastoise used an Ice Beam. A jet of ice hit my Exeggutor square on, hurling it against a nearby wall, freezing it in place, and causing my friends and I to fall down as Cora began to roll down the stairs.

'Cora!' I yelled as I saw her tumbling, out of control, down the spiral staircase.

The blow had been too damaging for my Exeggutor, who grew faint and disappeared back into my cell phone. Samuel and I jumped up and ran down to help Cora, who was lying in the corridor below, holding her right knee. The Blastoise, who was upstairs on the floor we'd just left, didn't seem to have finished its job, because it used its water jet against us, firing from the top of the stairs and pushing us further into the hallway with the force of its cannons. We were hurled against the wall.

'What now?!' shouted Samuel, coughing out the water he had swallowed. 'Why is it attacking us?'

'I don't know!' I yelled back, but I was focused on Cora, who didn't look good and had also swallowed a lot of water.

'Oh no,' Samuel muttered as he looked closer at her situation.

We heard a bang coming from the attic above.

'Cora, are you okay?' I asked, pushing the hair out of her face. She spat out water continuously.

'My knee and my shoulder are hurt badly,' she answered, coughing and writhing. I took a look and saw a sizeable cut on her knee.

A new blast came from above. Samuel and I looked at each other.

'Let's get her out of here!' he shouted, while what looked to be a flash flood started coming down the stairs in our direction.

We dragged Cora through the corridor and to the room where Blanche was hiding. Samuel slammed the door behind us.

'Phew!' we said at the same time, leaning on the closed door as we lay Cora gently on the floor.

At that moment, I knew what a real battle was like and what risks it involved. Many times before this, I had thought about how much fun it would be to live in the game, but now I was changing my opinions about many things that had happened in the last few days. It was almost 3:00 a.m., and we were in a deserted church, with a destructive Pokémon guarding the gym, in the company of a former team leader who was too afraid to do anything.

'What's the matter?' asked Blanche as she stood up quickly, obviously scared.

'Just a little problem with a Blastoise,' Samuel replied, sitting down on the floor, his arm still in the sweater sling.

I opened my backpack, grabbed the first-aid kit, and disinfected Cora's knee wound. Her trousers were torn right where she had sustained the cut.

'It's ... all ... right,' she quietly said, breathing deeply with each word. 'Just hurting ... a little.'

'A Blastoise?' Blanche yelled. 'He left a Blastoise to protect this place?' She came closer to us, grabbing Samuel by the shirt.

'Hey, what are you doing?' questioned Samuel, taking her hands off him.

Cora stood up, limping, and leaned against the wall beside Samuel.

'Blanche,' she spoke to the leader, 'who is this guy? How can he be so powerful?'

'You don't understand!' she said. Blanche anxiously walked in circles around the room. 'He is the last Pokémon Master! He's the only one left. He stole Pokémon from all over, until he had *all* of them in his power! Now no one can compete with him.'

'Wow!' Samuel exclaimed.

'And how did he bring you and the Pokémon over here, into our world?' Cora asked with her face contorted with pain.

'I don't know how he did it. And I don't know of anyone more powerful than he is,' concluded Blanche, turning to face Cora with a very serious expression.

It was Samuel's turn to ask a question. 'Did you get here yesterday?'

'Yes. I don't know for sure what happened, but one moment I was there, and the next I was here. It happened in the blink of an eye.'

'And have you also been here in this room since yesterday?' I asked.

'Yes. Ever since I appeared here and had to battle with this guy, I have been in this room. After my defeat, he stole all my Pokémon. ALL OF THEM! My poor Articuno ... This man, he can see everything. I have never come across anyone like this before.'

'How is this possible?' Samuel inquired, more to himself than Blanche. 'How did he bring the virtual world to the real world?' He started to breathe with difficulty, as though he was having an asthma attack. 'HOW IS IT POSSIBLE?' he shouted with his one good arm raised high in the air.

'Hey, take it easy,' said Cora.

'Nothing here makes sense!' Samuel shouted again, walking around. 'Perhaps,' he began thinking aloud, 'the universe is not only ONE universe, but a multiverse with an infinity of possible parallel universes,' he said, coming to a pause. 'And in one of these possible universes … the Pokémon exist!'

'*Samuel*!' shouted Cora, in an effort to stop Samuel's barely coherent chattering. But it didn't last long.

'OR ELSE THIS GUY USED A GENERATOR OF INFINITE IMPROBABILITY!' he continued. 'It's like in *The Hitchhiker's Guide to the Galaxy*!' Samuel, now panting with exhaustion, stopped speaking as his mind continued to try to make sense of it all before beginning to speak again: 'Or else … maybe we're all dead! There in the park, when those trees were falling on our heads. BAM! We all got struck by them, we died, and this is some sort of purgatory we've earned because … we bunked off school. And this is our punishment.'

Cora put a hand on his shoulder and, looking deeply into his eyes, said, 'Samuel, honey. Stop freaking out like this.' Then she turned to the other girl. 'And, Blanche, you'd better pull yourself together, too, because you're coming with us.'

The expression on the Mystic team leader's face was not encouraging at all.

# CHAPTER 16

# INFALLIBLE PLANS

For almost an hour, Cora had been trying to convince Blanche to leave the room. Needless to say that, at this point, she was pulling the fallen leader by the arms, despite being smaller than her and having an injured knee.

'I am not leaving here!' Blanche yelled and screamed ceaselessly. 'I don't want to die! This world is mad! I'm too young!' she repeated.

'Hey! Don't you get it? *We need your help*!' Cora shouted back.

I had been sitting against a wall for a long time, Samuel by my side, trying to think about anyone else's death but my own. That was my way of avoiding thinking of mine, which, in my opinion, would be slow and painful. Samuel, apparently, was still in a state of shock now that he had really stopped to examine the scientific side of the situation and couldn't find a convincing justification for it. All of this really shook his logical mind to the core.

'It's not possible to know what I'm going to find out there if I go. I will stay here, in safety, until I can find a way to get back home!' Blanche continued to cling to anything she found in the room while Cora kept pulling and pushing her.

'This is the part you don't understand!' Cora started shouting again. 'If you do not come with us, you'll never go back home! BECAUSE YOU WON'T SURVIVE!' she roared, both out of pain and rage. Cora had never been a very patient person.

'WE WILL ALL DIE! NOOO!' Blanche howled, and I covered my ears, trying to transport myself to another, easier point in my life, when Blanche and her cohorts only existed in the world of games. I tried to breathe slowly, letting the air invade my lungs.

Suddenly, Samuel stood up, walked up to Blanche in silence, and stopped right in front of her.

'Look,' he sighed. 'You have *no* choice. Either you come with us, or we'll make you come with us. Got it?'

Samuel was as tall as she was, and his tone was intimidating. The girl didn't answer, but she calmed down and followed Cora towards the door in silence.

'Take that, Pokémon players! And you thought team leaders were the only courageous people!' Cora said.

'Cora! Stop it,' I said. 'Of course she's afraid; she's in a new, unfamiliar place, totally different from what she's used to. Furthermore, everything she's had has been taken away. Let her feel fear if she needs to!'

Cora shrugged her shoulders, as she always did when someone challenged her.

We carefully walked down the corridor and went back to the church's nave, where masses were held.

'So?' I asked. 'What's the big plan that will save us all?'

'Cora and her infallible plans,' Samuel joked. 'Which generally fail.'

At this moment, I could imagine the smoke coming out of Cora's ears.

'Then why don't you think of something?!' Cora yelled as she charged at Samuel, pushing him against a wall with her face very close to his. 'If you're so clever! You could start being useful, too!'

I was scared with this new development. I had never seen my friends fighting in this way. I had to do something before everything went awry.

'Hey, please stop, you two! We have to work together!' I said, peeling Cora away from Samuel. 'Cora, can you explain your plan to us? Because I'm sure you have one.'

'When we were in the attic, I saw the Articuno through a window,' she confessed.

'I did, too, but how does that help us?' I asked, analysing Cora's expression for answers.

'This'll help us because you said the Articuno is one of the strongest Pokémon! And we're talking about one of the legendary birds, not just some ordinary creature!' she explained. Her eyes began to glitter with excitement.

Blanche joined us, with a wilting expression on her face.

'Great idea, dear. Though it seems you've forgotten that the Articuno DOES NOT BELONG TO ME ANYMORE!' Blanche shouted.

Cora brought her face very close to Blanche's, almost touching her chin.

'AND THAT'S WHY WE'RE GOING AFTER IT!' Cora shouted back at her, making Blanche very still.

'She may be right, Blanche,' I said. 'If the Last Master stole your Pokémon, we can do the same to him.'

Blanche looked at each of us with a frown on her face, pondering her decision. Then she took a deep breath.

'All right, let's go,' she agreed.

And with that, we all finally exited the church.

The Articuno had been circling the area for quite a while; we just had to wait for it to return to this part of the city. The problem was that the more the time passed, the closer the Last Master got to conquering another gym.

We sat down on the kerb, waiting. Cora began to engage in conversation about irrelevant subjects in an attempt to lighten the mood, but none of the conversations were sustained for very long. We were too tense for chit-chat.

Off in the distance moving silently to and fro, a Zapdos appeared, flying over the small buildings on the other side of town. We barely noticed it at first, and once we did, we didn't believe what we were seeing. The Zapdos was very large, and it left a yellow trail wherever it passed, like the tendrils of smoke squadron planes used to make. When the legendary bird was gone, my friends and I looked at each other for a long time. We were very worried.

The vision of the Zapdos confirmed one of our greatest fears: the Instinct team had been conquered. That meant the Last Master had succeeded in bringing its leader, Spark, to where we were. And worse still: he had beaten him. I could hear the ticking of a clock in my mind, telling me that time was running out. The Last Master had to conquer just one more gym, and it would all be over. And not in a good way.

Nobody said a word about this new development. I knew that Cora worked non-stop in trying to puzzle out the best strategy. I also knew that Samuel would seek a solution from the science books he continually read and memorised. I tried not to disturb either of them.

You know, when we grow up fearing certain things, we get used to it. I had long since reached a point where I'd stopped making an effort to try to ignore or run from these fears. And I wasn't even trying to be brave because I had already come to realise that I was not that kind of person.

But I couldn't go on like that anymore, could I? I had to overcome it. All of it. Even though I had been defeated in all the battles so far, even though nothing worked, the least I could do was try. Try for my family, try for my friends, who were there beside me, doing all they could to help me. I had to try just as hard as they were trying.

I stood up and started walking a little taller, looking intently up at the sky. Perhaps by coincidence – or was this possibly a sign? – when I looked up, I locked eyes with the legendary Articuno, that was now flying right over our heads.

'There!' I cried out. My friends all came to attention and looked in the direction where I was pointing.

'All right, Blanche,' Cora said to the leader. 'Get its attention!'

'I'm supposed to get … its … attention?' Blanche asked. '*Get its attention*?' She shouted this time, as if Cora had asked her to do something crazy, like performing a handstand on the surface of a moving river or something equally impossible.

Cora continued to stand there, looking awfully fed up with Blanche, who was now tearfully gazing skyward at her old friend. So Cora took a deep breath, let out a long sigh, and held Blanche's hands in her own.

'You want your friend back, don't you?' she asked, gripping the other girl's hands tighter. 'So make it see you. Make it remember that *you* are its true trainer!'

When the Mystic team leader looked up again, I have to admit: I started to believe.

# CHAPTER 17

# LOSING HOPE

I guess I could say it was magic, or some crazy natural phenomenon. Who knows? All I really can say with any certainty is that when Blanche looked up in a way that made the huge Articuno return her stare, something deep, something primal, seemed to have happened.

I really hoped the bird would recognise Blanche as its true trainer the moment it saw her, but if there's one thing I learned from all these experiences, it's that reality is never easy and, when things can be complicated, they invariably will be. This is almost a law of nature. Apparently, it holds true for Pokémon as well.

The Articuno hovered in the air as though it was analysing us, making the atmosphere around us cold and intimidating.

'Lucas?' Cora called to me. 'You'll have to give us a little help here. Which Pokémon would have an advantage over it?'

'Over a legendary bird?' I asked. 'It will wreak havoc on any of them, like Blastoise did with my Exeggutor!'

'Do you have a better idea?' Samuel asked.

Obviously I didn't have a better idea, so I grabbed my phone, accessed the app, and analysed my Pokémon collection, which was now almost complete. The Articuno was a creature of ice, and thus had cold winds swirling about it and around everything nearby. So the best I could do was to choose ... the Charmander.

'Okay, I know which one!' I said. 'Go, Charmander!' I touched its image in my collection.

'Fire against ice, hmmm?' Blanche commented, without taking her eyes off the Articuno. 'Not bad for a kid.'

This time, as it left the Poké Ball, the Charmander didn't look so ill-tempered – quite the opposite, in fact. It seemed glad to see us. I mean, until the moment it spotted the Articuno.

'Don't worry, Charmander. This is going to be easy,' I said as my Pokémon looked at me as though I had lost my marbles. I used all the stardust I had to increase its power.

'Hi, Charmander. How have you been?' Blanche started engaging with it. 'Look, this time your trainer is somewhat right, so take it easy. I know all about this Articuno, and I'm going to help, okay?'

'Charmander!' my Pokémon replied in agreement.

'Good! Let's go!' I said. I was excited. Despite being a little scared, if there was one thing that I liked about the game, it was the Pokémon battles, even though I ultimately preferred the virtual ones. 'Charmander, Flame Burst … now!' I shouted out.

The Charmander faced the bird, covered itself with flames, gathering as much power as possible, and then attacked with Flame Burst. The Articuno suffered a direct hit, becoming engulfed in a ball of fire and smoke.

'Great!' I celebrated.

'It would be so much easier if we just threw a Poké Ball to capture a Pokémon like in the game, wouldn't it?' Samuel asked.

'Unfortunately, reality has to complicate everything,' I answered, trying to assess the Articuno's situation. 'Everyone, watch out. Because there'll be a measure of revenge,' I warned.

The Charmander and I just stood there, waiting. The Articuno flew down to us, landing on the ground. Then it sent an Ice Beam toward my Pokémon. Despite Charmander being a Fire type, the Articuno's freezing breath was a critical blow for my Charmander, who was knocked out by it.

'No!' I shouted, running to help my Charmander. But it was too late. It had vanished back into the app.

Blanche approached her old Pokémon carefully.

'Hello, old friend! How are you?' she said to it. 'Are they treating you well?' She touched the blue bird's plumed head, which bent down to her. 'I know you are enjoying this world, but we need to go home. Don't you want to go home?' The Articuno made an indescribable sound in reply. 'I know you do,' Blanche continued with her sweet voice, while still stroking the bird.

I looked at the two of them, still upset because my Charmander had got hurt. I gave it a potion to aid its recovery, but I didn't move. My friends remained completely still as well.

'The Charmander really hurt you, didn't it?' Blanche asked the bird. 'It's all right. I'll give you a potion to make you feel better.'

Blanche turned to me, her hands still caressing her Articuno. 'He's coming with us, Lucas,' she said to me. 'Can you use a Poké Ball?'

'Okay,' I said, already opening the app. I threw a Poké Ball toward the bird. The Poké Ball hit the Articuno, bounced off of it, and then vanished into thin air. Nothing happened. 'I don't think it wants to go home,' I said.

'Look at it!' shouted Blanche. 'The thing it wants the most is to go home. It's just scared. I know my Pokémon!'

'She's right, Lucas,' Cora said. 'Pokémon don't go about simply attacking. They can be frightened, helpless creatures, too.'

I was quiet, thoughtful. Then I understood.

'Guys, the problem is the Poké Ball. A common Poké Ball won't work for a legendary Pokémon!' I shouted. Reaching back into the app, I threw a Great Ball next in the bird's direction. I really thought this would succeed, but again, nothing happened.

'It's hopeless,' said Samuel.

'There's only one way of capturing a legendary

Pokémon…' I started to say, but I never got a chance to finish because the game app, still open in my phone, had announced that I'd finally come to level fifty.

As you're probably aware, when we go up a level in the game, we earn some rewards. But I had no idea of what happened when level fifty was achieved, because I had never met anyone who had got there. However, I had just found out that level fifty afforded a player … a Master Ball.

'Today might be our lucky day,' I said, throwing the Master Ball toward the Articuno, who was immediately captured.Against a Master Ball, no Pokémon has a chance.

'Whoa,' Samuel uttered.

If that wasn't luck, then I don't know what was.

## CHAPTER 18

# NOTHING GOOD HAPPENS AFTER MIDNIGHT

The time to celebrate was short, so we did what we could, yelling and hugging one another and calling on the Charmander, Squirtle, and Bulbasaur to help celebrate. Even Blanche was excited now that her Articuno was safe.

'I'll return it to you,' I told her. 'You realise that, don't you?'

She gave me a hug, with an expression of pride on her face like the one my mother had when she saw a favourable school report.

'I know, boy,' she answered, letting go. 'This Articuno is very special.'

The four of us headed back to the attic, ready for a new battle against the Blastoise. It goes without saying that the victory was easy, since Articuno's attacks were much more powerful than the Exeggutor's, and demolished the massive monster.

We managed to retake the gym, and I left my Gyarados to defend it. The time had come to set off for the next battle.

Walking out through the church doors, we picked our bicycles up off the ground.

'Blanche, you can come back out now,' Cora said, already getting on her bike.

'Good luck to you,' said the leader, 'but I won't be accompanying you. Leaving that room was enough of an adventure for me. Don't get me wrong, but this world of yours scares me.'

Cora, Samuel, and I shrugged our shoulders, and Samuel got on the back of my bike. We waved goodbye to Blanche and rode off. The second gym conquered by the Last Master was at the municipal library, about six roads away from where we were. And we had to take it back from him before he took the third and final gym.

The deserted streets left the city with a sinister air. Usually in the middle of the night, some bars and shops remained open, but not now. After the world had gone haywire, the only visible lights at night-time were coming from just a few windows. It was eerily quiet. The entire city was shrouded in the deepest silence.

At the library, there was no light visible on any of the five floors. I think we were more worried with this gym, even after the victory against the Blastoise, because our town had many old urban legends involving the place.

You may think it's silly, but the truth is that no one dared stay at the library after darkness fell.

'All right, guys. Should we go in?' Cora asked, after realising that a good amount of time had already passed since we'd arrived and we were still sitting on the bicycles.

I remained on my bike, because despite feeling more secure about the whole saving-the-world thing, I was in no psychological condition to cope with the library in the middle of the night.

Samuel got off the back of my bicycle and joined Cora, who was already at the front door with her arms crossed and tapping her foot against the building's entrance. I looked up. Nothing could be seen through the windows above. The building, even in normal conditions, gave me the shivers. I sighed, got off the bicycle, and joined my friends.

'Ready?' asked Cora, uncrossing her arms and reaching for the doorknob.

'Wait a minute,' Samuel said, reaching into my backpack and grabbing a torch. He pressed a button and the light blinked several times before dying out.

'We'd better call the Charmander,' suggested Cora. So that's what I did. Moments later, it was back with us.

'Use your mobile phone torches,' I said. 'I won't use mine because the battery's only at half power since I used my extra charger a while back.'

'Watch out for Zubats!' Samuel advised.

Cora turned the doorknob and the door opened without any noise. We went in slowly, completely on alert. We passed the empty reception and the study room. In the back, where the first bookshelves were, we noticed a quick and subtle movement, which unnerved us.

When this kind of thing happens in situations like this, you can imagine that hearts race, eyes open wide, and people's bodies freeze into place, motionless. And that's just what happened. When we don't know who the enemies are, or where we are going to find them, any unknown noise will result in a tidal wave of fear. And the atmosphere of this place certainly didn't help.

Cora tried to calm us down. 'I bet there are only some Zubats here.'

I had no clue as to how she could remain relaxed in this situation.

'There may be some rats as well,' Samuel added. 'I doubt they clean this huge place very often. I heard that the council is bankrupt.'

We searched around the bookshelves, trying to find the Pokémon left there by the Last Master.

'This library is quite large; it may take a while before we determine the battleground,' Samuel whispered.

'Why are you whispering?' I asked him.

'I don't know. This place is so … quiet. I'm afraid if I speak too loud, I'll disturb someone … or something,' he said, looking towards the end of the corridor, where the history books were.

For a second, we saw a floating figure pass from side to side ahead of us. Cora, who was further ahead than Samuel and I, stopped dead. We remained quiet, but we didn't see or hear anything else.

'Don't you think we should split up to cover more ground?' suggested Cora.

'That never works in horror movies!' I answered. 'We're better off staying together.'

'You would know better, Chosen One,' Cora said as she shrugged her shoulders and walked away from me.

'Samuel, do you remember the story of the librarian?' I asked, now whispering myself.

'What librarian?' he inquired, looking at me with a raised eyebrow.

'The one who died here, many years ago, you know? It's said she never left the library.'

'The story I was told was about a child who came to pick out a book and died here. And how nobody could ever explain what happened afterwards,' Samuel said as we both began taking steps backwards, very slowly, one deliberate step after the other. The Charmander, who was behind us, also started to walk backwards.

'The story I know is the one about the librarian who was about to close and leave the library,' I said, 'and she was murdered. People heard shouts from the street, but when they got inside the building, she was dead and there was no sign of the murderer. They say she's still around here, and once in while, at night … you can hear her cries for help.'

'Lucas, I think we'd better stick to talking about Pokémon,' Samuel interjected.

The sound of something crawling on the floor made me and Samuel jump. This was easily turning into the longest night of my life. Then we heard Cora scream.

'Ahhh!'

We desperately looked around for her.

'Cora!' we cried out together.

'Where are you?' we kept shouting. 'CORA?!'

Samuel waved his phone around, looking around the library with the aid of his phone torch beam, but failed to find any sign of our friend.

'What do we do?' I asked, but Samuel didn't answer.

I had no idea why I had gone on and on about a murder story at a time like this.

# CHAPTER 19

# A TRUE
# HORROR STORY

The worst feeling that exists is the one you have when you realise you are inside a horror movie. It's really not pleasant at all.

We didn't hear anything else after Cora's cry, so Samuel and I started to walk, side by side, using the Charmander and the phone as our sources of light. I had the feeling that something was watching us.

'I am not liking this at all,' Samuel muttered. Our eyes and ears were wide open, searching for a sign of anything.

'Coraaa!' I shouted once again.

Nothing.

A figure off to our right passed by, moving towards some other bookshelves.

'Did you see that?' I asked.

'I wish I could say no, but...' Samuel replied. Our hands trembled and even the Charmander made weird sounds, looking worried.

'Let's keep searching,' I said. 'She has to be somewhere.'

'It's too dark, Lucas. This Charmander doesn't help as much as I would have thought.'

'Over there! Did you see? Over there!' I shouted.

Something had passed behind Samuel. I couldn't see clearly, but it looked like a person.

'There's someone over there, Samuel! Behind you!'

Whoever it was appeared close to us and grabbed my shoulder.

'Uhhhhhhhh...'

'AAAHHHHHHH!' we both screamed in abject terror.

'A-HA-HA-HA-HA-HA-HA!' Cora's laughter echoed across the enormous room full of bookshelves. 'Oh my God, you were so scared!' She leaned on me, with one hand on her belly, having a laughing attack. 'I thought you'd pee your pants!' she went on, tears rolling down her face. 'But now I think I will, from laughing so hard!'

Cora placed her hand on my arm, but I pushed it away. This girl had no common sense. She looked right at me, trying her best to suppress her laughter.

'Ah, you silly boys,' she said, drying her tears. 'I couldn't help myself. All these stories of murders and screaming. You are really silly to be afraid of such things. Those stories are just for scaring children.'

Samuel gave her a dirty look, then checked the time on his phone.

'It wasn't funny, Cora. The only thing you did was waste our time,' he replied.

'If you don't want to help, you could at least not get in the way!' I shouted.

Cora looked annoyed and crossed her arms.

'You're such idiots! Me? Get in the way? I don't know if you realise this, but *I'm* the one who's planning and keeping this all moving, okay?' she yelled with a stern voice. 'And I won't apologise for playing a silly prank.'

Samuel and I said nothing, because that is how we reacted when we were faced with truths we didn't want to hear.

'I think we'd better keep going,' said Samuel, and we resumed walking. We searched around the first floor and then headed towards the staircase to look upstairs.

'Let's hurry up so we can get out of here,' said Cora.

The municipal library had a wide, robust stairwell, an inheritance from the city's rich past. We climbed the steps feeling a little calmer, despite Cora's sick joke. I put away my mobile to save the battery and went ahead, breathing deeply and slowly to help calm myself.

I was beginning to think that it would indeed be faster if we separated, but fear prevented me from announcing this opinion. The library was even scarier than the church.

'Guys, I don't think we are being very smart here,' Samuel said, making us stop at the top of the marble stairs, right by the entrance to the second floor.

'Samuel,' I began to say, 'I never said we were—'

'—I'm serious,' Samuel cut in. 'Remember in the church,

how the place where the Blastoise was had the gym symbol – like a hologram? We are so dumb! I can't believe I didn't remember this!' He started speaking non-stop.

'What is it, Samuel? Just spit it out!' Cora said impatiently.

'A hologram, Cora! Holograms are made of light! Do you see any light on this floor?' he shouted.

Sometimes I feel really stupid.

The second floor was totally dark. Standing there, before an infinity of bookshelves, I was truly grateful to not have to thoroughly search every floor to discover our battle site.

'Ahh ... got it,' admitted Cora. 'Let's keep going up, then.' She continued to lead the way, with Samuel, the Charmander, and I following closely behind.

Climbing those stairs in the dark was pretty frightening, but when we got to the third floor, we saw, off in the distance between two bookcases, a pulsing light, which only escalated our fear.

'There!' shouted Cora. 'Come on!'

We raced towards the light, but when we were halfway there, it went out.

'I'm sure this is not a good thing,' Samuel whispered.

'Let's head back and go to the second floor,' said Cora, already turning around.

A figure passed by our side, making me jump. I looked ahead, to make sure Cora was there and it was not one of her jokes again. This time, it wasn't.

'Uh, guys? I saw something,' I said.

'You saw *what?*' Cora asked.

'A figure, or something. Just like I saw downstairs,' I added.

'Let's just keep on walking,' Samuel said. 'Let's think of rainbows, Clefairies, and cotton candy.'

We picked up the pace back to the staircase, but I was stopped by a floating phantom of a woman who appeared right by my side. She was wearing spectacles and carrying books. This time, what I saw was not a figure, but the perfect and ethereal form of a person, who must have haunted the place for a long, long time. When I found my voice again, after the immediate fright had passed, I could do only one thing:

'AAAAHHHHHHHHHHHH!' I yelled, and ran as fast as I could, trying to hide between some bookshelves.

'*Now* what is it?' Cora asked, but I didn't have an opportunity to answer, for the next thing I heard were Samuel and her shouting, and desperate footsteps echoing from all sides.

I hid under a table, between some shelves. I couldn't see anything, not even a few feet in front of my face. The sound of my friends' footsteps against the floor suddenly stopped as well.

Just as it always happened in horror movies, we'd been separated from each other.

## CHAPTER 20

# SOME TYPES OF POKÉMON ARE WORSE THAN OTHERS

I was absolutely sure it was a ghost. It was transparent and white as it floated by, and it perfectly matched the story of the librarian who everybody said haunted the place. I hid for a few minutes, hoping to hear something, anything, but there was no sign of my friends.

'Keep calm,' I said to myself, trying to work out what to do. I was panting because of the fear and the mad dash to this hiding spot. Gathering what little courage I still had, I got out from under the table and called out for my friends in a very low voice, practically a whisper. Nobody answered.

I had no idea which way they had gone, so I started walking slowly between some shelves that were cluttered with books. I peered from behind one of them and saw the supposed ghost there in the back of the library, merrily dancing from side to side as though she was playing. I sat down on the floor, trying to contain my fear, but got startled by the ring of my phone. It was Cora calling.

'Hello?' I answered.

'Lucas, where are you?' she asked anxiously. 'I found the hologram; it's on the top floor.'

'Hmmm, that's great. But I have a little problem down here,' I explained, swallowing those last few words.

'What's the matter?' she wanted to know, now sounding worried.

'It's the ghost … COMING RIGHT AT ME!'

I slid the phone back into my pocket. There was no time to run away now. The figure hovered above quietly, as though it was observing me. Then it started approaching me slowly, as if its main goal was to scare me as much as possible. I hugged my legs to my chest and closed my eyes, feeling tired and completely worn out. I could almost feel my body falling asleep.

'Lucas?' Cora called to me. I didn't answer. I just hugged my legs tighter; the sensation of falling asleep was passing. 'Lucas?' I felt something touching my hair. 'LUCAS!' This time, the shout nearly punctured my eardrums.

'C-C-Cora?' I asked, raising my face to meet hers, confused.

'Don't worry, the ghost is gone,' she answered.

I looked around to confirm this. Phew. There was no sign of the librarian ghost.

'Hey, come over here. I have to show you something,' she said, pulling me by the arm so that I stood up.

'What is it?' I asked, hoping my heart would resume its natural beating rhythm again.

'Can you see those purple lights up there?'

'More ghosts?' I asked, terrified.

'No. Just take a look. Let's get closer.'

'Get closer? Are you crazy?!'

'Trust me,' she replied, as if this made everything better.

I was too scared to object. Cora was taking me by the arm upstairs in the direction of the lights, which was near where the bookshelves ended, in the back of a room. I looked behind us at every step, with the constant feeling that someone was following me. So far, there was no sign of Samuel.

'It's so cold in here,' I said, hugging my body with my free arm.

At last we got close enough, and I finally realised what the source of the lights was. It was three Gastlys, those black balls surrounded by a purple haze, floating between bookshelves. One of them, when it noticed us staring at it, transformed immediately into the phantom woman I had encountered earlier, and passed above our heads.

'Oh, it's obvious!' I shouted, ducking beneath the 'ghost'. 'The Gastlys like to play tricks by transforming themselves into frightening things. I did see a purple figure passing down there,' I said, feeling quite foolish.

'Yes! Gastlys love to play such jokes on gamers,' agreed Cora. 'And the Last Master must know this as well, otherwise he wouldn't have placed them here.'

'Let's be careful with them. Their gas can make us faint

in a matter of seconds if we breathe in too much of it,' I warned, staring at those Pokémon with serious concern. One of those had almost scared me off. If it weren't for Cora...

'Did you happen to see Samuel and the Charmander?' she asked. I shrugged my shoulders. I hadn't even seen which direction they had run.

'Well, let's get away from these Gastlys,' she added. 'They're making me nervous.'

We walked around the whole floor and finally found the Charmander lying down quietly near the stairs, patiently waiting for us.

'Where's Samuel?' I asked it. The Charmander pointed upwards in the direction of the fourth floor. I looked behind me suddenly, once again feeling the sensation that someone was following us. It started to get colder, and my body began trembling like it had earlier in the church.

'Look, I didn't see anyone up on the fourth floor. I just came from there,' Cora said, already climbing the stairs and lighting the way with her phone. The Charmander and I followed her, almost running. We passed by the fourth floor, seeing the light of the gym hologram in the background. We continued going upstairs until we reached the fifth floor.

It was totally dark. There were no sounds, and every once in a while, I looked over my shoulder, still certain that something was behind me. This world full of Pokémon was really grating on my nerves.

'Samuel!' shouted Cora. As soon as we set foot on the

floor, we quickly hurried down a corridor and started looking at every space between the bookshelves we came to.

'SAMUEL!' she cried out again.

No answer.

With her phone's torch now pointing directly at me, Cora turned her head from left to right, analysing me.

'What is it?' I asked.

'Hmmm...' was all she would say. She had a hand on her chin, thinking about something she'd seen.

'What *is* it??' I insisted, growing more nervous.

'When I say 'now', you raise your arms as fast as you can, okay?' she asked.

I stared at Cora with a most alarmed expression. 'Are you serious?'

'Just do it, okay?' she reaffirmed. 'Now!'

I raised both my arms quickly, looking like a complete idiot.

'A-ha!' she screamed triumphantly. 'I knew there was something off here.'

'What was it?' I asked again, still in the dark about her discovery.

Cora came closer holding the torch, but I still couldn't understand what had just happened.

'Nothing much. It's just that there is a Gengar hiding in your shadow.'

'What??' I looked behind me and nearly jumped at the sight of my own shadow moving by itself.

As if it knew it had been discovered, the little red-eyed monster stood up and observed us with a malicious sneer.

'We'd better get out of here,' Cora advised.

# CHAPTER 21

# THE NEWEST PRISONER

Ghost-type Pokémon had just entered the catalogue of my most hated things, that is my 'blacklist'. What unbearable little creatures they were! Their pastimes were to scare us and make silly jokes. They were practically the Pokémon version of Cora.

We got away from the Gengar very quickly. The last thing we needed was to have problems with Ghost-type Pokémon. But I should add that their very existence was already a big problem.

While we walked between some bookshelves, Cora spoke about this type of little monster.

'In a way I like them,' she said. 'They really are lively. I still don't have a Gengar, myself. Do you think I should have captured that one?'

'Cora, however much you may identify with them,

I think you'd be better off catching a Gengar once things go back to normal, and they appear only in your phone. It's better not to deal with real-world ones for now.'

Cora seemed to reflect on the matter, finally agreeing to let those Pokémon stay where they were.

'I wonder what happened to Samuel...' I said, changing the subject.

'He was so scared that he may have run out of the library and left us here!' Cora joked.

'I thought Samuel didn't believe in ghosts,' I pondered, thinking aloud.

'Yeah, but he also didn't believe Pokémon could be real things. And yet, here we are.'

'Quite true,' I agreed.

When we walked further down the floor and saw no sign of our friend, we really started to worry.

'SAMUEEEEEEEEL!' Cora shouted out so loud that even the ghost Pokémon must have been frightened.

'Cora?' we heard a distant voice ask.

We ran up to a side wall where there were armchairs and tables. The Charmander arrived shortly, sliding its paws along on the waxed floor. We came across a most unusual sight: Samuel was partially hidden behind an armchair, in which sat a boy with spiky blond hair. The boy was tied up and gagged.

'Okay, now I really have seen it all,' said Cora, observing the scene.

'Samuel, get out of there,' I said, rolling my eyes.

'But what about the ghosts?' he asked, peering nervously from behind the armchair.

'There are no ghosts whatsoever, you fool. Those were only Gastlys mocking and making fun of us.'

'Gastlys?' he asked, looking very confused.

'Yeah, you know. They like to do this kind of thing,' I answered.

'So ghosts don't exist? Just Ghost ... Pokémon?' he asked, starting to piece it together.

'Exactly. So you can stand up and explain why you're keeping a hostage there in the armchair,' Cora ordered, crossing her arms and staring at the bound captive.

'I was using him as a human shield from ghosts; I couldn't let him loose,' Samuel replied, standing up and dusting off his trousers.

'That sounds like my friend,' I said, giving him a pat on the back.

Cora approached the boy and pulled off the gag, causing him to wince.

'Can you tell us your name, please?' she asked.

'Only if you stay away from me,' he answered.

The boy was older than us and was wearing a yellow uniform. I didn't need to hear his name to know who he was.

'For someone who's totally immobilised, you certainly are very courageous,' said Cora, approaching his face, bending over to get a closer look at him. 'Or you're very stupid.'

'I am Spark, leader of the Instinct team,' he replied.

'Leader?' I asked, and the boy turned away as if insulted by the term.

'Ex-leader,' Spark clarified.

So the Last Master had demolished one more leader. Reality then came back to hit me fully, reminding me that we had very little time left to make our world return to normal.

'What else have you got to say?' asked Cora, sitting down in one of the armchairs and looking at her fingernails as though she didn't have any other cares in the world.

'And why would I have something to tell you?' Spark replied, raising one of his eyebrows while looking disdainfully at his interrogator.

'Hey, big mouth, you are picking a fight with the *wrong* person!' said Samuel, looking at Spark and taking a seat in the armchair adjacent to Cora's.

'I think the fact that you are tied up, and we are the only people here who can let you loose must be a good incentive for you to open your mouth, wouldn't you say?' Cora inquired, as she walked over to Spark and patted him on the cheek.

'Yes, pal. This boldness and gung-ho pride isn't winning over our cold-hearted female friend here,' Samuel mocked.

I was tired of my friends' foolishness and jokes. We were wasting time with all this talk when we could have already explained the situation to Spark instead of making fun of him.

'Guys, let's let him loose; we have to go!' I said, pulling at the ropes binding his hands.

'Hey, Lucas. Wait a minute!' said Cora. 'Let him explain what happened. It might be the same thing that happened to Blanche.'

'You've seen Blanche?' he asked, growing scared.

'My friend, there's a lot about us that you don't know,' Samuel replied. He leaned on the boy's shoulder, but Spark promptly shook him off. 'Let's start with our names. I am Samuel, this is Lucas, and that's Cora.'

'We met Blanche after she was beaten by the Last Master and had her Pokémon stolen. With her help, we re-conquered the gym for the Mystic team and recaptured her Articuno. That's pretty much it,' I added, telling him everything that had happened as briefly as I could.

'Now we need to do the same thing around here,' said Cora, undoing the ties that held Spark.

We just had to find out which Pokémon we were about to fight next.

# CHAPTER 22

# THAT STINKS!

The more I found out about the Last Master, the more surreal everything seemed. Spark told us that the all-powerful Master was the only one capable of transitioning between the two worlds, the virtual and the real.

'This is madness,' Spark said to us. 'For me, what you call the "virtual world" is real life, not this barren, listless place you reside in.'

And the more I thought about his comment, the more I agreed. Reality is different for each of us.

Moreover, Spark's story was very similar to Blanche's. The Last Master was a known and feared character in the Pokémon world. One fine day, he met Spark and brought him here. I can't imagine how desperate he must have felt showing up here in our world. As with Blanche, he took away the leader's Pokémon, including the Zapdos. Then he tied and gagged Spark, and left a few ghost Pokémon around to scare away any potential rescue parties. Luckily for Spark we showed up; otherwise, who knows how long he would have been trapped here?

'This chat has been lovely,' Cora said, 'but we need to go up there, where the next hologram is.'

'Then let's go,' I agreed. 'Hey, does anybody have anything to eat?' Hunger pangs reminded me that I was starving. Samuel remarked that I had chocolate bars in my backpack, so I unzipped it and took one out.

We started walking back to the stairs and then we noticed that Spark wasn't following us.

'Hey, Spark, aren't you coming?' asked Samuel, looking over his shoulder.

'Oh, let me guess.' Cora put a hand on her chin, as though she was thinking. 'You don't want to go because you're scared to death and you think that children like us can't do anything to help you?'

Spark raised an eyebrow.

'Basically, yes,' he affirmed.

Cora sighed and rolled her eyes.

'Typical,' she muttered.

'You should know better, after all we've told you,' Samuel said, continuing to walk again. But soon afterwards, we heard the teenage leader's footsteps bounding up the stairs, following us. Cora laughed in a way that was characteristic of someone who knew they were right.

The top floor of the library was the most illuminated one, with a skylight on the ceiling that allowed light to enter so visitors could read. That late in the night, the moonlight was illuminating a large section of the room, so we didn't need the torches to guide us. There, the bookshelves were new, and the tables and chairs were quite comfortable, as everything on this floor had been renovated some five years ago. Previously, it used to be just an abandoned storeroom, full of old newspapers and moth-eaten books.

The gym hologram was in the right corner of the room, a dark and shining greyish symbol, indicating that the place belonged to the Last Master's dark team. I waited until everyone was together and took the phone out of my pocket. I touched the symbol on the screen, which rotated at the same time as the hologram in front of me did.

A Weezing appeared, with its two purple heads emitting weird sounds. As soon as we saw the poisonous Pokémon, we were hit with its horrible, putrid smell. I wished dearly that this type of Pokémon could only exist in my phone. We all covered our noses and mouths instantaneously.

'Eek, Lucas. This Pokémon is worse than one of your farts!' Samuel joked. I shot him an angry look. This certainly wasn't the right time for that sort of joke.

I was thinking of which Pokémon to use against the Weezing. Poisonous Pokémon were vulnerable to psychic Pokémon. I opened my collection of little monsters in the phone and considered my options. I had an Abra, a Hypno, a Drowzee, a Kadabra, and an Alakazam. I didn't have much time to formulate a proper strategy, but the best choice seemed to be the Alakazam. I touched the Pokémon's image and got ready for the battle.

'Alakazam, I choose you!' I screamed, and the Pokémon appeared in front of me.

The smell was still unbearable, and even the Alakazam was annoyed by it. The Weezing made a noise with its two mouths when it saw a fellow Pokémon before it. From my point of view, the two-headed monster had a tired look. I almost regretted having to battle against it.

My Pokémon was ready, so I kicked off the fight.

'Alakazam, Psycho Cut, now!' I shouted.

Two blades created by the Pokémon's psychic skills flew at and pierced the Weezing so fast that we didn't see it happen. The attack was devastating, since I had evolved the Alakazam and attained a very high Combat Power for it.

The Weezing threw a Sludge Bomb – a stinky explosive that appeared to be made of raw sewage – right over my Alakazam's head. My Alakazam lost its balance just as the bomb exploded and struck everyone in the room. I was sick to my stomach, with a feeling too disgusting to describe. The greenish-brown liquid dribbled over our clothes, and my friends' expressions indicated they were about to vomit.

The attack left my Alakazam vulnerable, but I still had a card to play. I thought of a new attack that would make the Weezing even weaker, and if my Alakazam remained strong, we would have a good chance of winning the battle by the third round.

'Alakazam, Shadow Ball!' I shouted. A black ball of dark matter crashed into the Weezing, cutting its energy bar in half. 'Way to go!' I shouted.

I turned to look at my friends, hoping for some encouragement, but all of them, including Spark and the Charmander, were too busy trying to rid themselves of the slimy liquid that blanketed all of us.

The Weezing faced us. I tried to anticipate what he would do next, but I couldn't decide what his best move would be.

The Pokémon's heads began to inflate and deflate over and over. This lasted for a few seconds, until a green gas, smelling even worse than the slimy liquid from the bomb, began to rise up and out of its heads.

At first I didn't understand what was happening, until Samuel's shout alerted me of the danger. In a matter of seconds, the green smoke started filling up the entire room.

# CHAPTER 23

# THE SPECIAL POWERS OF SCIENCE

**B**reathing poison gas is not a great experience. I hope you never experience this. It's not only the fact that these gases, well, cripple your senses and make you lose consciousness. They also really, really stink!

'Watch out!' shouted Samuel, pulling up his shirt to cover his face with it. 'The Weezing's gas is toxic! Try not to breathe!'

'Try not to breathe?' Spark asked, repeating Samuel's words as if he were crazy. Shortly afterwards, the Instinct leader fell on the floor, unconscious.

'What do we do now?' I shouted, though before I finished speaking, it was my Alakazam's turn to start looking a little woozy. Charmander wasn't looking so good either.

Taking in Samuel's expression, I could tell his scientific

brain was working at Mach speed. Until ... a great smile broke across his face as he seemed to have an idea.

'Cora! Call Bulbasaur now!' he yelled at the same time that Squirtle emerged inside the room.

Cora covered her face with a part of her coat that she had soaked in water from one of her bottles. She threw a little bottle to me, and I did the same.

'Bulbasaur, fetch something to break this skylight, quick!' ordered Samuel. Bulbasaur grabbed a wooden ladder leaning against one of the bookshelves and hurled it against the skylight in the ceiling, sending little glass shards raining down all over the place. 'Now, Charmander, set a fire there, right under the hole in the ceiling! Hurry up!'

My Pokémon staggered over and spat flames onto the floor, almost in front of the Weezing, who was still awaiting a new attack. 'Bulbasaur, break every window up here!' Samuel shouted.

I had no idea what Samuel was doing, but he looked quite determined, until he started to falter, his eyes seemingly getting awfully heavy all of a sudden.

'Guys, I'm not feeling very well,' he said, sitting down on the floor.

'No! Samuel, you cannot pass out! We can't do this without you,' I yelled, approaching him, panic-stricken.

'It's ... done,' he answered, and then collapsed down to the floor.

Then I realised that, little by little, the bad smell was going away. I looked up. The green smoke was being lifted to the top by the heat of the little fire made by the Charmander. Gradually, the Weezing's toxic gases were escaping through the broken skylight.

Cora took the water bottle and poured the rest of its contents on Spark's and Samuel's faces. My friend came to, coughing.

'Hey, , where did you get this idea from?' I asked him.

'He's a genius. You know how geniuses are; they get ideas out of thin air,' Cora answered.

'We did this experiment in my science class,' replied Samuel. 'Last week…'

'On second thoughts, maybe he's not a genius. I think he just has a very good memory.' Cora shrugged her shoulders, helping Spark back to his feet.

'Squirtle, put out the fire for us, please,' Samuel asked, and the little blue turtle launched a jet of water from its mouth to extinguish the blaze. 'When we don't have to fight against evil anymore, Pokémon might prove to make life much easier,' he remarked.

'Even so … what exactly did you do just now?' I enquired.

'A convection current,' Samuel answered very matter-of-factly. 'The fire warms up the air, the hot air goes up, and the cold air outside the library is sucked to the inside through the broken windows, as simple as that. It's just like a fireplace with a chimney.'

Cora and I looked at him without understanding how he found any part of that plan so simple. In the meantime, the Weezing continued to hover, looking even more tired.

Using the phone, I called my Hypno to the battle. It was now or never for me to take that gym back.

'Hypno,' I said. 'Psyshock, now!'

My Pokémon materialised a psycho wave that struck the Weezing, causing critical damage. The toxic monster fainted and the gym hologram changed from a dark to a light grey colour.

'We made it!' I shouted.

'Spark, it's up to you to take over this gym again,' Cora advised.

'I can't do that without any Pokémon,' he replied. 'The Master took away my Zapdos.'

'Oh, we're going to fix that,' Cora declared. And using my mobile, she set an Electabuzz to defend the gym for the time being. 'Done. Now this belongs to the Instinct again,' she declared triumphantly.

We were ready for a fresh plan.

# CHAPTER 24

# A HUGE DOSE OF REALITY

**W**e were outside the library, sitting on the doorsteps leading to the entrance, taking in the boredom of our still-quiet city with its abandoned cars and fallen trees, while we waited eagerly for the famous electrical bird. It was only a few hours before dawn, and despite it all, I still was able to wonder, rather fearfully, what would happen if my mother woke up and didn't find me at home. Perhaps I'd prefer the water jets and the toxic gases.

Perhaps.

Spark was eager to be reacquainted with his Pokémon friend, and I was getting ever more nervous that if we didn't settle this matter soon, we wouldn't arrive in time to prevent the Last Master from conquering the Valor team. The problem was that Zapdos never showed up when you wished them to, and we could do nothing but wait.

And I hate to wait.

After almost an hour, I had an epiphany.

'Guys,' I announced, 'get on your feet. I have an idea, and I think it's a good one.'

My three human comrades and the three Pokémon all stood up, looking at me.

'Cora and Samuel, call your Pikachus, please. And I'll call mine.'

'What do you want three Pikachus for?' asked Samuel, arching an eyebrow.

'Oh, you'll see!' I said excitedly, while I accessed the app and touched my Pikachu image. The Electric-type little rodents appeared together on the pavement, wearing confused expressions.

'Oh, just *look* at them,' Samuel spoke, his voice as sweet as that of an infatuated little girl. 'They're like triplets. I'll call them Theresa, Carla, and Renata,' he cooed, pointing to each of them.

'You dope, you don't even know if they are all female!' Cora pushed him lightly.

'They are too cute to be boys,' Samuel concluded. If this had been a cartoon, Samuel's eyes would be big, beating hearts.

While those two discussed Pokémon gender definitions, I touched the Articuno's image, liberating the ice bird, who seemed to appreciate being free again in our world. It shook all over as though it were waking up from a deep sleep.

'Articuno, I'm sorry to bother you, but we need your

help,' I told it. 'We need you to use your Blizzard attack and aim it directly at the sky.'

The ice bird swung its wings slowly, accumulating enough energy until they formed a little snowstorm. Then it took off towards the heavens, unleashing a mess of water, wind, and ice everywhere. The nearby clouds were sucked in by the slow whirlpool produced by the Articuno, and it transformed the sky above us into a great storm without any lightning or thunder. And this was the problem the Electric rats would solve. My Pokémon knowledge reminded me that Zapdos appear during thunderstorms.

'Attention, Pikachus,' I said, making them look at me. 'Thunder Shock!' I shouted. (I had always wanted to say those words!)

The three Pokémon all closed their eyes, making a conscious group effort, and suddenly directed electrical bolts towards the falling rain improvised by the Articuno. Shortly after that, we had a storm with lightning and thunder.

'Done!' I said to my friends. Cora was speechless, not fully understanding the thunderstorm's origin, and Samuel wasn't even paying attention, as he was too busy hugging the Pikachus. I could see their little yellow faces growing more strained and begging to go back to their respective Poké Balls.

Spark walked over and stayed beside me, looking at the dark sky. It was only a matter of seconds before the Zapdos emerged and flew headlong into the storm.

'Articuno! Come back here!' I shouted, and the blue bird touched down on the pavement. Meanwhile, the Zapdos kept crossing through the clouds, gaining energy from the electricity.

'Now we just need to get its attention,' said Cora.

Spark started shouting for the bird, but it was too far overhead to hear its trainer's call. Then I made a decision, and it was a rather risky one, but time was slipping away and our chances of defeating the Master were shrinking every moment. I needed to stop thinking and act.

'Pikachu,' I said, addressing the little female Pokémon. 'It's time to use your Thunder Shock once again.' I pointed to the Zapdos in the clouds.

The little female Pikachu, as Samuel insisted they were, were rather soundless. I think they had already realised that my suggestion was going to cause us real trouble. But nevertheless, they launched a Thunder Shock.

The Zapdos, upon getting struck by the Pikachus's electric bolt, was quite upset with them. Although the attack was harmless, it annoyed the bird, which plunged down out of the air, heading straight in our direction.

'Well, I think I got what I wanted,' Samuel muttered as he saw the winged Pokémon approaching.

'Oh no,' I said to myself.

The Zapdos hovered in the air about ten feet off the ground, observing us. As the Pikachus who attacked it trembled with fear, Samuel, Cora, and I called them back to their Poké Balls, but this didn't improve the bird's mood.

'Lucas, I think you'd better think of something fast, because it's preparing to attack!' Spark shouted nearly in my ear.

'Speak to it!' I replied.

'Zapdos! It's me!' Spark yelled, but the Pokémon didn't seem to understand. 'I don't think it works this way,' he muttered to me as he gave a fake smile to his old friend.

'All of you, call your Pokémon back and get in that car, now!' Samuel shouted, pointing to an abandoned car in the middle of the street. Quickly, I sent Charmander and Articuno back into the game app and raced into the car, following Spark, Cora, and Samuel.

We squeezed inside, without understanding what we had accomplished in following Samuel.

'I have to tell you guys – I don't know how to drive,' declared Cora.

'Stop messing around, Cora,' I replied. 'We're not driving anywhere … are we?' I turned to look at Samuel.

'Be quiet and do not touch the doors, steering wheel, or front console!' Samuel shouted out at the very instant the Zapdos sent a very powerful electric current our way. Ah, it was the famous Discharge attack.

I waited for my life to pass before my eyes, but nothing happened.

'Lucas, send the Master Ball now!' Spark advised. I hurriedly fished my phone out of my pocket and launched a ball toward the Zapdos before it decided to attack again.

The ball caught fire and quickly closed the distance

between its target. It shook once, twice, three times ... and the Zapdos was captured.

We had passed the second stage.

# CHAPTER 25

# IF YOU PLAY WITH FIRE, YOU'RE GOING TO GET BURNED

I can't say I enjoy going to school, but going back there in these conditions somehow made everything even worse. There were so many actual gyms to choose from; why did the Last Master have to pick the one at my school? I imagined the havoc he must have wreaked in that place already.

At least we lived in a small town, which meant that we could get fairly quickly by bicycle to all these places that the Last Master had corrupted. I cycled at the fastest speed I could, and the going was much quicker because of the still-deserted streets. However, we had barely arrived at the school before we came face-to-face with a problem that was very … big!

A Snorlax was sleeping in front of the school's gates, blocking the entrance.

'You've gotta be joking,' grumbled Cora, observing the Snorlax's fat belly going up and down in time with its deep and calm breathing.

'We'd better hope the back gate is open,' said Samuel. 'I hope it's not too dark inside there, because my phone battery is now toast. That's what you get when using it as a torch all night!' he complained as we ran around the block to get to the back of the school.

'My battery is running low, too,' commented Cora, with worry trickling into her voice. 'Lucas, you'd better use yours only if it's absolutely necessary, okay?' she asked, and I nodded, touching my pocket to make sure my phone was securely in place.

We arrived at the rear of the school, but that gate was locked, too. Suffice it to say, today wasn't our lucky day.

'Yup, I knew it,' said Cora. 'They usually lock it all up after the rubbish has been taken out and the school van drivers have finished work for the day.'

'But both the church and the library were unlocked! Why is this different?' I asked, feeling discouraged.

'I think it's because the owners of private schools have more appreciation for the safety of their assets.'

'Yes,' Samuel agreed. 'The library is a public domain…'

I took the phone out of my pocket. The school's gym still belonged to the Valor team, but time was running out, so we had to rush.

We went back to the gate where the Snorlax was fast asleep. I stood there examining the tranquil beast, failing to find a solution.

131

'What are we going to do?' Samuel asked. 'Wake it up?'

'Believe me, you do *not* want to wake up a Snorlax,' I cautioned him.

'So then what? Shall we sit tight in the hope that some other supernatural being will show up to solve our problem?' he pleaded, upset.

'You still haven't accepted the fact that things have radically changed, have you? You have to think outside the box now,' said Cora, speaking in a way that made us look like two creatures without functioning brains. So she grabbed her phone and brought the faithful Bulbasaur back to us.

As soon as I saw the small Pokémon, I felt truly stupid. With its vines, it scooped us up and nimbly set us down on the other side of the school fence.

We were in.

We proceeded down the school ramp until we came to the front doors, which luckily weren't locked. We then walked around dark corridors, opening the doors of some classrooms to check if there was anyone around, but found nothing. Some rooms were in disarray, with broken desks and rubbish strewn around. And on some walls, charred black streaks indicated that some fire Pokémon had been there. We crossed the school grounds, where we came across a group of Rattatas, who ran away as soon as they saw us – which was great, because a Rattata's bite is notoriously painful.

'Guys, I think I found what we're looking for,' said Cora,

who was up ahead of us and in the school's courtyard, pointing at a figure in the distance.

We saw a tall man wearing a black shirt and black trousers, who was facing a black girl with short hair, who was dressed in red and white clothes. But we couldn't concern ourselves with who we were certain was the so-called Last Master, because at the end of the corridor, a visibly upset Dragonite blocked the passage to the courtyard.

It was a pattern that had continually played itself out all night: whenever we thought we were close to recognising a problem, or, even more so when we were trying to solve it, something came up to make things much more complicated. We even blamed ourselves for having complained about the earlier situation, not knowing how much more dire it would soon become.

As soon as it saw us, the Dragonite delivered a jet of flames in our direction, which didn't miss us by very much. Not very much at all.

'AAAH!' I shouted, stamping out a fire that had started on the tip of one of my trainers. 'Why is it attacking?! Dragonites are kind and altruistic and they like saving people, not killing them!'

'Sure, but your other average Dragonite were not trained by the Last Master,' Samuel remarked, facing the giant Pokémon.

'So this one has good reason to be amped up,' completed Cora.

'Okay, fine. But what now?' I asked fearfully, taking my

phone out to see which Pokémon could help us with this new threat.

Nobody had the chance to answer my question, because our conversation had apparently made the orange dragon even more nervous. He launched a second jet of fire – possibly a flamethrower attack – exactly where we were standing. We managed to jump out of the way and tumble to the ground to avoid being burned … at least to avoid being *completely* burned. The trouble was, as I jumped my phone fell out of my hands, slid on the ground away from me, and ended up right beside the foot of the furious Dragonite.

'Argh! Now we really are done for!' Cora said, holding up her smoking arm that had been singed by the dragon's fire.

'Is everyone okay?' I asked, falling deeper into the grip of fear. We were hiding behind some pillars in the corridor, trying to protect ourselves from the heat of the flame attacks.

'I'm still alive, right?! But we have no way out of this situation!' she shouted, showing me her phone. 'My battery's at zero!'

'Take it easy, I might have some juice in my extra charger after all. Just wait.' I tried to calm her down, opening my backpack and handing her the device.

'For goodness' sake, Lucas! It doesn't help! Your phone is newer than mine, so the cable plug is different! What are we going to do?' she asked, her eyes wide open.

'Technology can be such a pain!' Samuel exclaimed,

squatting behind a pillar on the other side of the corridor from us.

We were so close to saving the world! I couldn't believe things were going to end like this.

## CHAPTER 26

# AN UNAVOIDABLE MEETING

**W**ith help from Pokémon, the solutions are always easier. We succeed in breaking things, going over sleeping Snorlaxes, and going about delivering Thunder Shocks and the like. But when their help is not available anymore, things can get unimaginably difficult. Especially if you are trying to save the world.

One of the main problems facing us was that we needed my phone to defeat the Last Master. Another problem was that the Dragonite had spat out so much fire in our direction that the floor all around us was burning.

It's a universally accepted truth that situations such as this justify moments of desperation involving crying, shouting, swearwords, and socially unacceptable behaviour. So along those lines, please allow me to say that, yes, I cried my fair share of tears, screamed, and swore. I cried out of tiredness and frustration, because I had been so close and things had been going well up to that point, and for this all to get nipped in the bud – a bud that was slowly getting engulfed in flames – well…

Even Cora, who always had a solution for every problem, was clueless. I was quiet, leaning on the pillar, finally, totally defeated. And then an alarm screeched in our ears, and water began to fall from the ceiling, extinguishing the fire on the floors of the corridor. Samuel had triggered the fire alarm.

'This should put out the fire,' said Samuel from the other side of the corridor, still hiding from the Dragonite. 'I don't know if it'll help us much, and remember that the floor will continue to be hot, so be careful.'

'Well, it's a start,' said Cora.

We waited until the flames were completely extinguished before peering out from behind our pillars. But just as before, we still saw ourselves in a dead end from which we couldn't escape.

After spending some time admiring the embers crackling, I turned towards Samuel.

'And now?' I asked him.

'What, Lucas?'

'Have you got any more ideas?' I enquired. In the distance, I could see Moltres, Candela's fire bird, hovering above her in the school's courtyard.

'Look, I do have something,' he said. 'But you're not

going to like it, and I won't be the guinea pig for trying it out.'

'Let's hear it, Samuel!' Cora screamed.

'Have you ever watched those videos on the Internet of people from India walking on hot coals?' he asked as Cora and I nodded. 'So this is *theoretically* possible, then?'

'Are you really sure about this?' injected Cora.

'This is physics, my dear. You can trust physics,' Samuel answered confidently.

In reality, this is an *incredibly* dangerous thing to do, and I know for sure that no one should ever, ever try it at home for fun.

Cora turned the idea over in her head and stared down at the embers again. As for me, I wanted to walk on the hot embers and save the world, I really did. The problem was that I couldn't get myself to do it. The gap between wanting to do something potentially dangerous and psyching yourself up to actually do it was very large. At least it was for me.

Cora stood up and looked at the embers scattered about the ground, setting her jaw with a firm resolve.

'You'd better be right, Samuel!' she said, looking at my friend again.

'Are you really going to do this?' I enquired, scared to death for her.

'Do we have any other option?' she asked, to which I shook my head.

'Cora, the Dragonite looks distracted – you'd better go

now,' Samuel advised. 'But remember one thing: walk, do NOT run!'

'Right, right. Walk, don't run—'

'—At a steady, constant speed,' Samuel completed her sentence. He walked over to her, grabbing her by the arm. 'And just one thing: you'd better go barefoot. Your trainers could melt and the fried rubber might burn your feet badly.'

'What?! You must be joking,' muttered Cora, already taking off her trainers. Then she went to the middle of the corridor and took her first step.

Samuel and I held our breath.

Cora didn't shout, which I took as a good signal, and continued, one step after the other, going across the ember-covered floor. Indeed, it seemed to me that anyone who was more courageous than this girl had yet to be born.

The Dragonite noticed Cora's presence once she got close to my displaced phone. We were panic-stricken as we watched the dragon spit more fire in her direction, but Cora was quick, and the Pokémon was large and awkward in its movements. She grabbed the phone, rushed to the end of the corridor, and hid behind the wall.

A few moments later, three of my water Pokémon emerged and completely doused the crackling embers.

'Cora! Summon Articuno!' I shouted, and using my mobile, Cora complied.

'Oh, yeah!' Samuel said, feeling encouraged again.

'Articuno, Ice Beam, now!' I shouted, and the Pokémon cast a wave of ice towards the Dragonite while Samuel and I raced over the ashes of the recently smouldering wood.

We joined Cora, stopping for a moment to catch our breath, and then we all ran again towards the school's courtyard.

The final battle was at hand.

# CHAPTER 27

# A CONTEMPTIBLE BEING

The thought of being face-to-face with the Last Master made me shiver, but for the first time, I didn't think of running away. All we had done so far had been leading up to this moment. I was scared, but I felt ready for the confrontation. And if by any chance we didn't succeed, at least I would know that we had done our best. It felt good, despite everything.

We ran so fast that we almost couldn't come to a stop when we reached the courtyard. Articuno flew behind us, keeping guard and watching over us from above. When she saw the ice bird, Candela, the beautiful leader of the Valor team, she let out a smile.

The Last Master, who was further back in the courtyard, observed us with a curious expression. He was an older man, about fifty years old perhaps, with jet-black hair.

His clothes were all equally black and looked like those of a successful businessman. He had nothing in his hands but a mobile phone. If I saw him on the street, I'd never have thought he was the villain trying to use Pokémon to dominate this reality. Positioned on either side of him were an Arcanine and a Lapras, set up there as bodyguards.

Candela's fire bird gave off a screech when it recognised Articuno's presence, as though it was greeting an old friend. Seeing this reaction, I grabbed my phone that was recently recovered by Cora and liberated Spark's Zapdos, too. The three legendary birds were now reunited.

Being in this courtyard was like being in an arena. But it didn't feel normal, it was more like being in a dream. I kept needing to remind myself that this was real, that everything up to this point had actually happened.

When we walked deeper into the courtyard and joined Candela, the Last Master finally spoke, saying:

'I have to tell you, children. I didn't think you'd make it this far. I thought these Pokémon were better warriors … But it doesn't matter; the best is yet to come.' He spoke slowly, in an easy manner, as though the thought of not defeating us had never crossed his mind.

None of us said a thing, we just looked at him. What I felt, as a matter of fact, was something close to pity. I don't know what could have made him believe that he was the all-powerful being of not only one, but two worlds. While I trembled with anxiety, I also considered the fact that it might be horrible to be the Last Master.

'What's the matter? You don't feel like talking?' he asked.

Cora snorted, losing her temper with the so-called Master.

'We are not here to talk, oh "Last Master",' Cora said. 'We are here to end this and go back home in peace.'

'Preferably with the city intact,' completed Samuel.

Standing before us, the Last Master smiled.

'I like you, girl,' he said. 'But I heard that the great hero here is Lucas, the most – how shall I put it? – skilled player of the three of you.' He faced me, fixing me with a rather penetrating stare.

I contained my fear, took a step forward, and glared right back at him.

'What is all this for? What have you got against our world?' I asked, my eyes still glued to his.

'Oh, I am from your world, my dear Lucas. And I was very happy in it, until … well, things got somewhat complicated,' the Master answered.

'But … how was it that you came to be in the virtual world?' I asked, becoming scared by the realisation that this guy might once have been someone just like me.

'I'm not only the Last Pokémon Master that was left, but I am also an excellent programmer,' he replied.

Samuel moved closer to him, looking at the Master with a curious expression. 'Did you really find a way of traversing between the real world and the virtual world? If so, this will change the world as we know it!' he almost shouted, becoming enthusiastic.

'Oh, but it has already changed,' the villain added with a smile. 'You have no idea.'

The way he smiled chilled me to the bone.

'Can we cut to the chase here?' Cora shouted. 'The more time that passes, the more these Pokémon will go about doing whatever they want to do with our world.'

'It's not just that,' Candela spoke for the first time, interrupting Cora. 'They are scared, desperate; they don't know what to do in this world. That's why there were so many accidents and destruction. These Pokémon want to go back home.'

'Wait a minute!' It was Samuel's turn to interrupt. 'So these Pokémon are real? Truly real? They don't just appear in our world through a game app? They are actually … *alive* somewhere?'

'Your world is a mirror of my world,' Candela said. 'From the moment this 'game' as you call it, was created, my world came to exist in reality in just the same way as yours has.'

'Wow. That's it!' Samuel said, more to himself than to anyone else. 'All the possibilities of multiple universes exist!'

'Guys, need I remind you that this man who's standing right in front of us wants to destroy everything and then conquer the world? This world and the other one!' Cora yelled, shoving Samuel and me very hard.

'He knows how to move from one world to the other, Cora!' I shouted back. 'What can we do to fight that?!'

'I don't know! But this is terrible!' she shouted, waving

her arms. 'And we still have to find some way to stop him!'

She was right. No matter what, we still had to take away the power he had in our world. But how? How could we prevent the inventor, the creator of the game who was also a programming genius, from doing whatever he wished with what he himself had discovered and created? He could probably dispose of us at any moment. Wasn't it the right time to run?

Cora stamped on the ground.

'We are going to use the legendary birds to do away with these little monsters,' she said, gesturing at the Master's Lapras and Arcanine.

'If only we could study this guy's brain before they take him away to jail,' Samuel mused.

'Very well,' I said, facing Candela, who returned my steely gaze of resolve. 'Articuno, Zapdos, let's show this man what you can do when you are with a *real* trainer.'

'Don't make me laugh, kid,' the Master answered.

If I survived the night, I reckoned that I'd probably go on to live for at least one hundred-and-fifty years.

# CHAPTER 28

# A NUMBER OF UNFORTUNATE REVELATIONS

**D**awn was already breaking when we began the battle. My forehead was sweating so much it was beyond control. Candela was by my side at the ready to act, facing the man that had plucked her out of her reality. I couldn't imagine how hard it must have been for her and the other team leaders to be taken from her world and thrown into an unknown one without any explanation.

'Are you ready?' I asked. Candela nodded and then looked at her Moltres in the sky.

I took a deep breath. If we didn't succeed, I had no idea what would happen. I held my mobile phone tightly with both hands, as though doing so would grant me some sort of mystical power.

Look, I thought to myself. The guy might be many things: a genius, a scientist, an all-powerful figure in the realm of computer science. But a Pokémon Master, he wasn't. I was pretty sure of that.

'Articuno, focus on the Arcanine and leave the Lapras for the Zapdos,' I said, without taking my eyes off the Master. We didn't have any true advantage that I could pinpoint. And that worried me a bit.

'Moltres!' Candela shouted. 'Fire Blast, now!'

The bird swooped low over our heads and launched a jet of flames onto the Lapras. The Pokémon was burned, but not damaged badly enough to affect it seriously, I didn't think.

'Articuno!' It was my turn to shout. 'Blizzard!'

The Arcanine had fully absorbed the blizzard, weakening the fire Pokémon. Next, Candela's Moltres, despite not having an advantage against either of the two opponents, dived right into the Lapras head-on, wreaking havoc.

I began to feel sick to my stomach. This didn't make sense. It was too … easy, I suppose you could say. In no time, both of the Pokémon who were guarding the Master had been defeated by us, without inflicting any serious damage to our three birds.

'Congratulations, children,' said the Master as soon as his Pokémon vanished after failing to withstand our attack. 'Did you enjoy playing?' he asked.

I was speechless, looking at Cora and Samuel. I had no clue what this man would do next.

'You don't even care if your Pokémon are wounded?' I asked. 'What kind of trainer are you?'

'I have no time for your foolishness, boy. I'd like to

know what you are doing here, challenging me. It has been fun, although it is growing tiresome,' he said. 'But it takes quite some time defeating the leaders, taking your gyms ... Well, you understand of course.'

'Head offices?' Samuel muttered to Candela, trying to grasp what the Master was alluding to.

'My world is a mirror of yours,' Candela repeated. 'There, we have the head gyms, where Blanche, Spark, and I stay, where we lead our teams. When the Master brought us here, we fell upon these same places, your world's version of our gyms, which, for me, is exactly where this school is. Unfortunately, if he succeeds in gaining control of the three gyms, then he will have conquered all the three teams and ... Well, I think you already understand.'

Samuel opened his mouth, astonished by all the new information.

'I hope you've enjoyed your time with the Pokémon,' said the Last Master, 'because I have to send them to the other side. You've wasted too much of my time already.'

'WHAT??' all three of us shouted at the same time.

You wouldn't want to see how badly us three desperate children reacted.

'Enough of torturing these kids, Zanke,' an unfamiliar voice interrupted.

A man, who was even older than the Master, with spiky grey hair and wearing a black-and-green uniform beneath a white coat, approached us from behind.

'I never expected to see your face again, Professor Willow,' said the Last Master.

Our jaws opened and fell straight onto the ground, just like in the cartoons.

'And I could say the same,' said Willow. Then he turned to the leader by our side. 'Hello, Candela. I'm glad to see you are well.' Candela nodded and smiled, happy to be with the Professor again.

I didn't know which surprised me more: the unannounced arrival of the famous professor, or the fact that he and Candela already knew one another.

'Oh, for heaven's sake, what's going on here?' Cora asked the Professor directly.

He got closer to her and reached out a hand.

'It's a pleasure to finally meet you, Miss Cora,' the Professor said, giving Cora a firm handshake.

'Same to you,' she told him, 'but let's cut out the polite formalities. Please, can you just explain what the situation is here?'

'Yes, I think it's time, isn't it?' he said to her, smiling before turning his gaze back on the Master, or 'Zanke', as he had just called him. 'But don't worry. Nobody from this world is going to the other world today.'

'Ah, my sweet Willow, how dearly I've missed your resolve,' Zanke said as he started walking in circles around the courtyard.

The two men's stares began to harden as they stared furiously at each other.

'But where do you know one another from?' Samuel

149

entered the conversation, curious to find out the story of the pair's past.

'We met long ago, Samuel, when we were still in college. We even founded a business together. It's a pity I was not able to understand Zanke's true character back then. Quite a pity,' he started explaining.

'But of course, now's the time to reveal each other's true characters,' the Last Master said. 'Let's just remember the fact that this dear friend of yours, children, imprisoned me in the digital world. I was trapped there for five years! FIVE YEARS, Willow!' he shouted at the other man, taking a few steps towards the Professor. 'And you dare discuss *character* with me?'

Appalled by this revelation, my friends, Candela, and I looked at Willow with new eyes. If what Zanke had said was true, then the Professor was the one who was chiefly to blame for everything that had happened.

'Professor Willow?' Candela asked, giving him an inquisitive look.

'I am not a bad man,' he answered, turning to face her. 'I did what I did because I saw no other way. He was jeopardising this world, and everyone in it.'

'Don't be pathetic,' Zanke snarled. 'It was that closed little mind of yours that was unable to see beyond the obvious, always fraught with too many fears, too many doubts. "Think of the risks, Zanke!" you always said. But, Willow, don't you realise that it's from risks that all great revolutions are born? Of course not! You were never able to understand that!' he shouted.

'We were not prepared, Zanke,' Willow shouted back. 'We still aren't prepared now. Can't you see what you're doing? This city is completely destroyed!'

I was following their conversation intently, trying to fish out bits of information as it went along, but too many pieces of the puzzle were missing for me to grasp the whole picture. What I knew in all certainty was that there was clearly a long history between these two. And I wanted to listen to every little snippet of it.

# CHAPTER 29

# A MOST UNWELCOME GUEST

**S**ome stories are so fantastic that we can hardly believe they're true. I guess I shouldn't be too surprised, because the story I, myself, was living at that moment was about as crazy as the one these two men were about to tell us.

The shouting between them was ceaseless, almost like watching my grandparents arguing over which TV channel to watch. Thankfully, Zanke and Willow's argument was a little more relevant to things that mattered.

'It needn't be this way,' Zanke said, pointing a finger in Willow's face. 'Things could have been different.'

'You created this game and you couldn't help but get carried away with all of it! You didn't care if the whole world was jeopardised with our discoveries. It wasn't the right time,' Willow answered back.

'But you decided this year was the right time, didn't you? How much money have you earned launching the app that I developed?' Zanke asked, confusing me even more. Surely *they* – the two of them – were the developers of the game? Weren't they?

'The app that *we* developed, Zanke, the both of us,' Willow went on. 'And your half of the money is being looked after safely, waiting to be given back to you on the day when you recovered, when you finally understood. This game, as it stands, is very different from what you wanted it to be.'

'Too late, my friend,' Zanke announced. 'I am now the Last Pokémon Master, the only one in the two worlds. And I will continue to be.'

Moving away from us, going towards the far end of the courtyard, Zanke looked at us with fury.

'I am sorry, kids. I didn't want it to end up like this for you,' the Last Master said. 'But I have no more time or patience for this matter.'

Then he took a mobile phone out of his pocket, a much bigger device than the smartphones we used, and with a touch, he brought to our world something I thought I'd never see. A Mewtwo appeared before our eyes. Its face burned with livid focus as it slashed its huge tail about aggressively.

I started walking backwards, very slowly. My game knowledge made me realise that there was nothing we could do. This was the most powerful Pokémon of them all, infamous for being completely devoid of any compassion. He would surely do away with us instantly.

'Zanke!' Professor Willow cried out when he saw the Mewtwo. 'You'll destroy us all! We had agreed to never let a Mewtwo out of the game!'

'That was before,' the Last Master shot back. 'Now I have become not only the *last* Master, but the *greatest* Master of every and any world. And Mewtwo is one of my servants.'

Professor Willow motioned us to move as far away as possible from the lethal Pokémon creature.

'Lucas, prepare your birds and call upon whoever you think could aid us,' he commanded. 'But always let Mewtwo attack first.'

Samuel and Cora stood nearby, observing the situation without knowing what to do. I think Cora saw the panic on my face, because she grabbed me and hugged me tightly.

'You will succeed, Lucas. You always do,' she said, letting go of the hug and going back to Samuel's side.

I grabbed my phone and I called Charmander into our improvised battle arena. I tried to remember what I knew about Mewtwo. It had been created by genetic engineering, was always focused one hundred per cent on its enemy, was cold and without emotion, and thought only of winning. By my calculations, we could well have to say goodbye to our little world.

Professor Willow noticed I was losing hope. He walked over to me and touched my shoulder. 'Lucas, you may be just a boy, and you may not have succeeded yet in capturing all the Pokémon, but you are already a Master. Of this, I am sure,' he said.

I nodded by reflex, not knowing if I entirely agreed with him or not.

Mewtwo began moving and I stiffened up.

The three legendary birds glided above us, and Mewtwo looked at them and licked its lips as if they were dinner. The birds were still quiet, waiting on Candela's and my commands.

Then, very matter-of-factly, Mewtwo levitated, rising to the same height as the other three Pokémon. Suddenly, a fierce commotion broke out up in the air. I then realised what was happening: the three birds were fighting against each other, fixated on killing one another, and not attacking the Mewtwo.

'NO!' I shouted. Mewtwo continued in the same position, its eyes focused on the three battling Pokémon. 'STOP! Please, stop! You're going to kill them' I kept on shouting desperately. Mewtwo looked at me for a moment, twisting its head slightly to one side, as though it could not understand what such an inferior being could be trying to do. I looked back at the birds, who were disoriented and savage. Looking over, I could see that Candela's hands had been tied up, too. 'Professor! Help us!' I shouted again, but I could see by his expression that nothing could be done to stop the aerial battle. The Mewtwo controlled the minds of those Pokémon, making them attack one another, so I had to find a way to disturb it and break its concentration.

'Lucas!' shouted Samuel. 'Let's get the heck out of here! Now!'

I saw him clutching Cora's arm, pulling her toward the courtyard's exit.

I looked at my friends. Out of options, there was nothing more they could do. But maybe I could still try one last thing...

'Charmander!' I shouted. 'Flamethrower, NOW!'

Charmander looked at me for a second, just to be sure that this was what I really wanted. Then it attacked. It launched its jet fire right into the belly of Mewtwo, who lost focus of the legendary birds and descended slowly to the ground. However, apart from momentarily ignoring the Pokémon above, it didn't seem to have been affected much by the attack.

Mewtwo observed Charmander with its complete attention.

'Charmander?' said my Pokémon. Its voice was insecure when it looked at me. Its expression was sad.

Then I saw what it was seeing. Mewtwo was resolutely locked in on it. It only took seconds to attack Charmander fully with its psychic cut. Its psychic blades were too much for Charmander, bringing it to the ground only a few feet from where I stood.

The Last Master observed everything with a sickening awe, like a proud father watching his son's triumph. I ran to Charmander, bent over it, and held it in my arms. It was unconscious, its breathing slow and light.

'No,' I said, the tears falling as I could do nothing to help it. 'Charmander...' I sobbed. Cora and Samuel ran over to us.

From the other side of the courtyard, Mewtwo watched everything with mild interest. The birds had disbanded and were now resting on the ground, exhausted and clearly injured.

The Last Master approached his Pokémon.

'Mewtwo,' he said. 'Finish the job now, please.'

We all looked at him, fearing the worst.

# CHAPTER 30

# A NEW WORLD

**H**owever gloomy certain moments may be, they are a little easier to deal with when our friends are around. Samuel and Cora held me while I cradled Charmander, who was motionless in my arms.

The Last Master commanded Mewtwo to attack us. The moment we most feared had finally arrived. But at least we were still together, as it should be. We closed our eyes and waited. At that moment tears were rolling down our cheeks.

A few seconds elapsed and nothing happened.

Mewtwo didn't attack. We opened our eyes and it only gazed at us, looking puzzled.

'Mewtwo!' the Last Master ordered. 'Attack them! Now!'

But again, nothing happened.

The Last Master's expression changed from triumph to fear in a matter of moments.

Then, just as suddenly, Zanke fell to the ground. His body struggled, breaking out into a convulsion, and his eyes rolled back into his head.

'What's happening?' Cora said as she took in the scene.

Professor Willow ran to help Zanke. Mewtwo's eyes were fixated on the writhing man.

'Zanke?' Willow called, taking the Master's face in his hands. 'Zanke!'

Willow grabbed the Master's phone off the ground where he had dropped it in the ordeal.

'Children! Move back!' he shouted. I carried Charmander, and the four of us squeezed into one of the alcoves of the courtyard.

Mewtwo stopped whatever it was doing and looked at us again. I saw its eyes fixed on Charmander, who was still in my arms. Then it saw Candela beside the Moltres, trying to calm it down. Next, it faced the Professor.

Willow accessed the app and cast a Poké Ball toward Mewtwo. The Pokémon continued looking at him, its eyes a little more serene as it was taken to the safety of a familiar environment.

It took us some time to understand that the threat had passed. Then we walked slowly up to the Professor, and Candela joined us.

'What happened?' I asked the Professor, standing at his side.

He looked at me and let out a sigh.

'Mewtwo cannot be controlled, Lucas. Zanke was very stupid to think his power was above a creature such as that,' said the Professor, checking the Last Master's pulse.

'But I still don't understand. Why didn't Mewtwo just do away with us?' I wanted to know.

'Mewtwo is a cold creature, at first sight. And extremely powerful. It is the final weapon, and it appears to hate humans because of what they did to it,' the Professor started to explain. 'But deep inside, it does have compassion, although it doesn't quite understand humans' relationship with Pokémon. However, the important thing to understand here is that Mewtwo saw something in you, Lucas. In you and in how you were behaving towards your injured Charmander, and this disconcerted it somewhat. Because of that, it formed a new opinion of our species.'

I took a deep breath, pressing Charmander against my body. Then I looked at the man who was lying unconscious on the ground, completely vulnerable.

'Will he be okay?' I asked, looking him over.

'Yes. The same goes for your Charmander, after you give it one of your revives,' he said, looking at the Pokémon in my hands.

Using my phone, I sent it back to the app and restored its health.

'What are you going to do with this guy?' Cora asked, walking over to us.

'I'm going to find a safe place for him, where I can make him understand that the greed for power always leads to disaster,' Willow explained, laying Zanke's arm gently on the ground. 'And most importantly, a place where he cannot hurt anyone else.'

I checked the clock on my phone. It was almost seven-thirty; my parents would be awake soon.

'Well, what happens now?' I asked.

'Zanke's "mobile phone" is going to take us away from your world,' Willow explained. 'As Samuel might have worked out by now, our bodies are composed of codes.'

'The genetic code?' Samuel completed.

'Exactly. This device, which looks like a phone to you, also works as a scanner of codes. Do you understand? It copies our information and returns it to the other side.'

'Because ultimately, we are beings who are composed of information! Like in *Tron*!' Samuel exclaimed.

'Exactly, Samuel,' the Professor agreed. 'Just like in *Tron*.'

Professor Willow stood up and cleaned his hands on his white coat, which was not that white anymore.

'The time to bid farewell has come, my friends,' he announced.

Candela gave each of us a hug. 'Thank you for everything. We will never forget you.'

I looked at the legendary birds behind us and the other assorted Pokémon nearby.

'Then ... we will never see them again?' I asked. 'Charmander, Squirtle, Bulbasaur?'

Willow approached me and bent forward to look me directly in the eyes.

'No, not in this way,' he answered. 'What you

witnessed here should never happen again. At least, not this early, not before everyone is prepared to deal with the consequences. That's what Zanke never understood.' Professor Willow put his hands on my shoulders, standing up straight before me. 'But your Charmander will always be with you. You know that, right? He will always be your friend.' He smiled.

Then, in a matter of seconds, Candela and the three birds disappeared, as though they had never existed in this world.

'Are you going to return Articuno and Zapdos to Blanche and Spark?' Cora added from behind us.

'Indeed, that's going to be the first thing I do,' Professor Willow answered. 'Oh, before I forget. I have something for you.' He slid a hand into his coat pocket. 'Ah, where are they, where are...?' he said, searching another pocket. 'Ah, here they are!' he said. 'It's just a gift, you know? Some souvenirs of what we experienced here.'

The Professor approached us and hung little medals around Samuel and Cora's chests.

SAMUEL
KNOWLEDGE

CORA
COURAGE

'And thank you very much, Lucas. For having gone ahead, despite your fears and everything else you endured. Do you know why you made it? Why you were able to accomplish all this?' the Professor asked.

I gazed at him, breathing deeply. Then I looked at Cora and Samuel, and smiled.

'Yes, I do,' I answered, and took my friends' hands in mine. 'It's because, unlike the Last Master, I didn't fight alone.'

Professor Willow smiled for a second before he vanished.

In my pocket, the mobile phone vibrated. I opened the app to see a new message.

Congratulations! You won a medal.

You are now a Pokémon Master.

# GOODBYE, TRAINER

Thank you for following me in this journey. I hope this has given you a better idea of what it means to be a real Pokémon Master. Perhaps I have succeeded in convincing you to change your mind and leave this crazy idea of playing with Pokémon behind. Parachuting is much safer.

But if you're seeking something other than safety, then I hope this story has opened your mind to many new ideas. One of them, indeed the one I think is the most important, is the certainty that anything, and absolutely everything, is possible.

Goodbye, trainer. I hope we meet again very soon.

# ACKNOWLEDGMENTS

I want to say thanks to Arnaud and Rejane, for always saying yes to my wildest ideas; to Paula Pimenta, without you, this book and many other things would not be possible; to Ale Starling, for the beautiful cover illustration; to Guilherme Fagundes, for the care and patience used to ensure everything turned out beautiful; to Renata and Jim, for improving the text; to Luciana, for seeing that everything was finished in time; and to my parents, for understanding how crazy it was to write this story and for having been so patient with me.

A special thanks goes to Armando, who helped me with new ideas and all the other scientific concepts used by Samuel in this book. You are a superb fiancé.